Mississippi Dreamer

Living Life on the Edge

The Street life to getting to know Christ

Jeremiah Barnett, Ph.D.

ISBN: 9781075915758

DEDICATION

I would like to give God, through Jesus Christ, all the Glory for my accomplishments. I would also like to acknowledge four special people who are no longer here with me but are here in spirit: Johnny Barnett, Johnny Nehemiah Barnett, James Pate, and Elsena Jones. They helped me understand the true meaning of strength and endurance through all situations. I would like to send a special dedication to my mother Barbara Barnett, who always listens to me and loves me unconditionally.

CONTENTS

ACKNOWLEDGMENTS

I would like to first acknowledge God, through Jesus Christ, for giving me the strength to endure this process. I want to thank Shenna Edwards for her editing expertise and insight. I want to give a special acknowledgment to my mother Barbara Barnett, who has always encouraged me, given me feedback, and demonstrated unconditional love. I would like to thank my family and friends for their support.

INTRODUCTION

The purpose of this book is to share my revelation about myself, Jeremiah Barnett. I was sent from Chicago, Illinois to Lexington, Mississippi and faced adversity daily. This book will exemplify and validate how God, through Jesus Christ, can change our current situations with prayer, fasting, and being obedient. In life, we deal with stress daily and do not understand how we get ourselves into certain situations. I will summarize this book by asking you to close your eyes and imagine growing up in Chicago with urine in the elevators, the crack house around the corner, shootings every night, and people at the corner store begging for money.

Think about it: the only professional you have ever encountered as a child is the teacher at the school. Ask yourself this question: "How can I be successful?" Growing up, every kid in my neighborhood had dreams of being a pro basketball player, football player, or a rapper. I asked myself the question over and over again: "Why is it that no one ever mentioned being a lawyer, teacher, business owner, or doctor?" As a young man in my community, it was not realistic to think that way because we had never seen a lawyer or doctor.

Introduction to Mississippi Dreams: Personal Story

On my way to my work in Chicago one hot summer day, the security guard in my building told me that my best friend, Larry, had been shot in the head the previous night and was on life support. I was in a state of shock. He was 16 years old and his mother's only son. I went everywhere with my best friend. His life ended because someone was shooting and made a mistake and shot the wrong person. The young man, Devon, who murdered my partner, turned himself in and told the police that Larry was his partner and he'd made a vital mistake. It was a senseless death. Devon was shooting at other gang affiliates in our community over territory and respect.

Consequently, I saw individuals at a young age going to prison and dying over gang signs and neighborhood nonsense every day. Meanwhile, the shootings and murders got worse. Most definitely, my family made up in their minds to send me to Lexington, Mississippi after Larry's death. At the end of the summer, I moved to Lexington, which had a population of 1,500 people. I lived with my grandmother in a shotgun house. Once you entered the front of the house, the first thing you noticed was the back door.

Moving from Chicago to Lexington was different. Everything was slower in Mississippi. There was only one red light and one stop sign in the entire city.

My dreams were cloudy and dark when I was at a young age in 1989. On top of that, I had to deal with segregation in Lexington. The African American children went to Jacob J. McClain High School and the Caucasian children went to Central Holmes Academy.

This book will elaborate on how being resilient and focusing on the calling of God drove me to the point of understanding my self-identity. At a young age, the mindset and the atmosphere of my surroundings kept me in a confused state of mind. Speaking about this will allow individuals to think rationally and logically to overcome the generational curses and focus on God as our number one source. This book will target several areas such as gang violence, relationships, understanding the importance of entrepreneurship, having an intimate relationship with God, and recognizing the covenant of marriage. This book's primary focus is to illustrate how having a close relationship with God trumps everything else in life. There are obstacles that we try to overcome by pulling ourselves out of the triangle of life without getting any guidance from God through Jesus Christ.

Understanding the Mind

In summary, our body cannot move without our mind operating. Furthermore, when something is not performing, it is powerless. Our intention is defined as the thought process and the characteristics of a person. Now, when our thought process is telling us we cannot do something and we cannot improve life's situation, we usually get into a distorted state of mind. Cognitive distortions are ways that our mind influences us to believe something that isn't true. These mistaken thoughts are generally used to strengthen negative thinking or emotions. For example, emotional reasoning simulates your negative emotions essentially. Negative emotions reproduce the condition of your mindset that produces the thought process of how you feel.

Consequently, our negative thinking controls our emotions to the point where we cannot get out of the bed, we isolate ourselves, and sometimes we are pushed to the end of giving up on life. When a person gets in the mindset of a depressed stage or an "I cannot do it" stage, they appear to become extremely cognitively impaired. They give up on life, dreams, goals, aspirations, and sometimes get to the point of not wanting to live.

CHAPTER 1

SEEKING THE WRONG ATTENTION

Introducing Living Life on the Edge

Close your eyes and imagine living in a world the prison population has cultivated. The entitlement of the disqualified population has grown, and the disqualified population is also made up of predominantly young, poor, black males. The prison incarceration of several black men decreases their life endeavors. When the majority of the black males are being institutionalized, it damages the financial lifestyle of the African American communities, diminishes public involvement, and stimulates alienations.

I, Jeremiah Barnett, walked in the hospital on a hot humid day in July of 1992. It was exceedingly crowded. I noticed gang members crying, screaming, and using profane language in the narrow hallway as I walked into the hospital room. I was in a state of shock. There he was, lying in the bed on life support. Wow! I had a paradigm shift that day—living life on the edge.

18 Years Earlier

I was born in Chicago, Illinois in 1974 when gasoline was $0.59 per gallon, milk was $1.65 a gallon and the nation was in the middle of a recession. As the years progressed, the murder rate increased in Chicago and the gang violence was on the rise.

First Introduction to a Police Officer

On a cold rainy night, at the age of four, I had my first encounter with a police officer. I went into the greasy corner barbecue rib shack with my mother's friend, Mary, around 10:00 at night. Mary was a thick, brown-skinned African American woman who could catch a man's eye with one glimpse. Yes, she was a sight to see. I noticed a tall, white, skinny police officer with a grumpy frown on his face. He had a toothpick in his mouth and was peeking at Mary's beautiful skin. Mary ignored him with a superficial smirk. The police officer screamed at Mary, "Are you this child's mother?"

Mary answered in a low-pitched voice, "I am not his mother, but his mother is around the corner."

The officer said, with indignation and rage, "I am going to take you and the child downtown with me to the police station."

Mary's voice pitch instantly got hysterically louder. She said, "No, I can take him to his mother." She shouted, "Please … please, Officer, don't take my friend's son!"

My mother saw us and started walking extremely quickly toward us, sweat pouring down her face. The officer grabbed his holster with a blank facial expression. My mother shouted, "Where are you going with my baby?"

The police officer told my mother, "I was two minutes away from taking your son and this young lady downtown to the police station." The police officer spit a nasty slobbery toothpick out of his mouth. He continued on to say, "This child is out after curfew and she is not his biological parent."

My mother was shaking with uncontrollable sweat. She replied with an exceedingly saddened face, "Officer, I am so sorry, and this situation won't happened again. I promise."

The police officer said, "Ma'am, I am giving you a direct warning. If I see him out here this late without you again, I am taking you to jail."

I immediately said, "You are not going to take my mother to jail—or anywhere else." I spoke about ten profane curse words to the officer in one sentence. In my community, during this stage of my life, it seemed like every-other disgusting unpalatable word that came out of people's mouths was explicitly foul language. I thought that using profanity was a way to express myself when someone offended me.

The officer said to me, in a calm voice, "Little Man, your mother is not going to jail." Then he walked toward me and shook my hand. Then he walked away.

When the officer exited the scene, my mother put me in the car and said, "You should never talk to anyone like that, especially the police."

I said, "But Momma, I was taking up for you. That mean officer was going to take you to jail."

My sweet mother said, "I can handle my problems … and you stop using all that profane language."

Loving Family

My birth mother's name is Barbara. I remember her pretty, silky-smooth skin. She smelled like fresh strawberries. Her eyes were light blue—like the ocean—and she had caramel skin and long legs. My father's name was Johnny Sr., and everyone called him "Hook." My father, Hook, was high-yellow with light brown eyes. Yes, surely, he was a ladies' man and my mother were well aware of his smooth ways. Hook was a "Cool Daddy" who knew how to diffuse a situation. As a teenager, I lacked the drive to become even unpretentiously successful, let alone become a prominent figure in counseling and the realm of higher education.

Pimp Tragedy

In 1982, there was a pimp named Slick who lived in my community. He used to have at least five females with him every time I saw him. Slick was a tall, skinny, fast-talker who always rhymed and walked with a limp. He used to call me "Li Man." Slick gave me two crispy dollars every time he saw me. Slick also had a red 1976 Cadillac Coupe de Ville that he custom designed. That was *one* clean ride.

He had one female named Ebony with whom he spent most of his time, outside of the other five females. One warm night, my older cousin Chris and I were walking on Madison Street in Chicago. Out of nowhere, Slick pulled up in his red Coupe de Ville, bobbing his head to some old-school funky music. He got out of the car wearing a shiny green suit with some green and white shoes to match. Ebony got out of the car and said, "Daddy, what you need me to get out of the store?"

He said, "A pack of cigarettes."

She smiled and said, "I will be right back, Daddy."

I spoke to Slick with a smile. He reached down in his pocket and gave me those two crispy dollars. I grabbed the two dollars and told my cousin Chris that Slick was a nice man. I did not understand why the people in the community always said bad things about him.

By this time, a pimp named Tony had pulled up on the scene. He was wearing a red and black suit. He started walking towards Slick pointing his finger. He screamed and said, "Hey Player, I heard you were trying to cop my b***h!"

Slick said, "I know this n****r not talking to me!" At this time, Ebony was walking towards Slick with a drink in her hand.

Chris and I were standing in front of the store on the wall when Tony pulled out a gun and commenced to shooting towards Slick. I witnessed my first murder at the age of eight. Everyone started running and ducking. I heard females screaming and horns blowing as people were trying to leave the area quickly. Once the smoke cleared, I looked down and saw Ebony, unconscious, with blood coming out her mouth.

Later that day, I found out that Ebony had died from a gunshot wound to the chest. My heart dropped, I thought pimps were cool until I saw Ebony die. I could not understand how she was selling her precious body and taking a chance on losing her life for a lousy dollar. I watched Slick for months looking sad and disappointed. He seemed lost and did not know how to express himself. Slick tried to be hard, but his emotions were connected to Ebony.

Even though he tried to put his feelings on ice, it did not work. Eventually, Slick stopped coming around the store and I heard he went to jail. I said to myself that I wanted more out of life, and that there has to be a better way out. I learned from my encounters with the pimps in my community that they are some lonely individuals who have had some painful life experiences. It seems like they had problems with trust and the fear of commitment at a young age.

I was ear hustling one night and heard Chris telling his homeboy Jeff something so ironic and weird. He stated that Slick's mother and father were killed by Slick's mother's pimp. I was in a state of shock, but I could not say anything because I did not want them to know I was listening. He also said, "Slick's daddy was a complete lame and used to cry and beg his mother to stop selling her body and stay at home." Chris laughed out loud and said, "That is why that dude does not care and act so cold towards those women—because he never wanted to end up like his daddy."

The street put me on a fast track at the age of eight. Slick's tragedy with his mother was similar to his tragedy with Ebony. Instead of his wife getting murdered by a pimp, his prostitute was killed by a pimp. I saw a community lost in a culture of violence and I never could understand why.

Family Time

I evaluated my life after that horrible tragedy with Ebony and Slick. I realized that I was the only child chosen to live with my grandmother out of five siblings. I thought my siblings and parents did not care for me because I was given to my grandmother to be raised. All of that time as a child, I sensed that I was alone on a ship with no real support.

I was extremely wrong! They did care, but I made up in my curious mind for many years that they did not care. My mother was the care giver and my father made just enough money to pay all the bills; it was exceptionally rough on my family. My grandmother was a blessing to give my mother assistance by raising me. Everyone called my grandmother "Big Ma." Her eyes were light brown, like a gift to the world. Her skin was brown like her eyes, with a glamorous, smooth surface. Her thoughts were like a clear, deep ocean that never stops flowing.

Whenever I was with Big Ma, I felt calm and safe. Big Ma did not take anything off of anyone when it came to her grandson, Precious. "Precious" is my middle name. She loved calling me her "Precious Baby." She worked for an older man named Mr. Eddie, cleaning up his fancy house. My siblings occasionally stayed with Big Ma on the weekends.

Whenever my siblings visited Big Ma's house, upsetting them was my number one priority to get their unwanted attention. My mother and Big Ma functioned as one terrific team to raise me. I remember every time my mother had extra funds; she would always purchase the latest pair of Jordan shoes with a matching jacket for me. She did that from time to time. We were unfortunate, but I could not tell because my parents' love covered all the powerless pain I saw in my community.

Introduction to the Projects

Big Ma and I lived on Warren Boulevard, down the street from the Chicago Bulls stadium. The projects were around the corner from my house and that was the place to hang out. There were several brown buildings with the smell of urine on the floors in the elevators, filthy paper all over the grass, and graffiti all over the walls.

The projects were ghetto fun. We protected our community with little effort from the police. The police always showed up twenty minutes after a shooting. As a young child, I figured that the police were waiting until the shooting was over. My little partners, Bullet and Nose, were Mr. Eddie's grandchildren.

They used to laugh and throw rocks at the cars that drove through our community. My parents lived across town on St. Louis and Huron for about three years. Around this time—I was about nine years old—I would get very upset with my grandmother because I wanted to stay at my mother's house with my siblings. My parents did not want me to leave, but my Big Ma wanted me to stay with her.

Big Ma was not going to let anyone keep me. She used to say that I was an exceptional child who needed her undivided attention. I would always ask my Big Ma why I had to leave my mother's house. She told me, "The doctor told me that you had a nervous heart, and I was helping your mother out." She would slowly gravitate towards me to give me a hug. She always said, "You require lots of attention, Baby."

I was uncontrollable and acted out for attention from my siblings. When I went to my mother's house, I used to go into my brother's clean room and leave everything in disarray. Johnny, my brother, was two years older than I was. He was wise and alert. Johnny was medium height, 5'11," with gray eyes and always had a cologne smell on him. In any situation, he always thought rationally before he reacted.

Attention Seeking

Being rebellious as a child, I felt like I was not getting attention from my primary caretakers, so I acted out by exploiting something that generated considerable commotion. I caused an evasive confusion to seek attention, regardless of whether it was negative. I did not know how to express myself positively, so I demonstrated negative attention-seeking behaviors. I had a strong, intense demand for attention. I was trying to figure out how to deal with my life. Therefore, I pushed situations to the limit for any reaction.

I was really unmanageable as a child, but the one thing that always was consistent was that my family continually operated in unconditional love. My mother finally moved to Harris and Human, on the West Side of Chicago, to a two-story apartment.

One day, I was outside bouncing my basketball and four young teens about five years older than I was asked to see my basketball. One of the teenagers looked really sneaky as he was walking towards me, but I still let them see the ball. They ran away with it. I chased them for a minute and then I went in the house and told my cousin Vincent.

Vincent always liked to tell jokes. Big Ma had adopted him, so we were like brothers because we stayed in the same house with Big Ma. He was my Uncle Charles' son. We went looking for them but could not find those thieves anywhere. I was mad that some teenagers would take my basketball. I was only ten years old. Vincent and I were walking back to the house and I remembered telling him that this was a cruel world.

I looked Vincent in the eyes, punching my fists together and stating that I was going to stay two steps ahead of anyone that was trying to trick me by not smiling and out-thinking them. I learned that day never to trust anyone with my basketball and always to follow my first instinct.

I also learned at an early age that respect is given, but trust is earned. My Big Ma allowed me to go and stay with my mother for the summer. I packed some clothes and was ready to be with my siblings.

The next day, my mother came home upset, stating that my father got into an aggressive altercation with a dangerous motorcycle gang. I remember her saying that they were going to bomb our house. My mother packed some things up for us and we went to my grandmother's house. I had just left; I really didn't want to go back so soon. My father stayed at home by himself without any fear. Once we went back home, my father told us that no one had come by our house.

He explained that we should never let anyone run us off from our home. My father was a man who would not let anyone bother his family. He demonstrated manhood daily. The way my father cared for my mother and his children was something special that I would never forget. He had a love for my mother that never ended. He would always kiss my mother and call her "Baby." It was always funny to me. My mother smiled and said, "Stop, Hook" when he started saying mushy stuff.

My mother enjoyed my father's smooth and charismatic words, but she always played hard to get. They were a God-sent couple who worked very well together. My father gave my mother his check and he kept his side-hustle money from odd jobs. They had something that money could not buy; it was **TRUST.** About four years later, we moved to the North Side of Chicago.

We moved to 4640 North Sheridan Road in a building on the 13th floor. While my mother was still in the Windy City of Chicago, Big Ma decided to move to the cultured country of Lexington, Mississippi. I was 12 years old and she wanted to create a better life for me and to change my environment. Big Ma received a small $86 welfare check each month to take care of me. She gave me $43 and she kept the other half. Big Ma and I lived off of those funds for an entire month in a green shotgun house.

The kitchen was the first room in the house, and it had a round white table. The house had one bathroom with three bedrooms and no dining area. My partners and I used to hang out in the kitchen. Big Ma's shotgun house smelled like greens, black-eyed peas, cornbread, and ham. All my partners used to love to come by Big Ma's house because she fed the entire community. Big Ma was a beautiful woman who loved children.

Racism in the South

My parents provided me with clothes each month to help Big Ma while I was in the Deep South of Mississippi. In Lexington, the town had only one red light and one stop sign in the entire city. My dream was cloudy and dark at a young age. In 1989, Lexington, Mississippi was a segregated town as well.

The African American children went to Jacob J. McClain High School and the Caucasians went to Central Holmes Academy. I walked by Central Holmes Academy every day and never went on that school campus. My partners and I were nervous and scared to go onto Central Holmes Academy's campus. We could feel the negative stares from the students. Unfortunately, I did not know how to communicate with different races because I was not around any other culture, race, or ethnicity.

On a chilly Halloween night, my partners and I were beatboxing and singing "I'm Bad" by L.L. Cool J. Out of nowhere, a white truck pulled up with about seven white young men on the back of the truck. They were chasing us with eggs and hitting us, saying "Nigga!" I started running extremely fast, but they were bigger and faster than I was.

I remember falling and one tall, white, skinny young man looked at me and said "Smile, Nigga!" while hitting me across the head. Once they left, my partners and I were upset and wishing we were older, stronger, and taller. It was like we were in a pool of water and drowning, and no one was near enough to save us. We were defenseless children in a racist society.

Crack in the '80s

There was the sight of horses and cows, and everybody spoke to one another in Mississippi. By comparison, if you spoke to someone in Chicago, they thought you had a problem with them. If you spoke to someone in Mississippi, it was known as a common courtesy. Around the corner from my green shotgun house there was a basketball court, the local neighborhood store, and the crack house. We called our neighborhood the "School House Bottom." One night I'd heard my cousin saying, "Reese killed his grandmother because she did not give him any freaking money for some drugs."

Reese was a young man who converted from a flawless high school football star to another victim of the hard-core and harmful drug—crack cocaine. That night, I told myself I would never want to be around a drug that is strong enough to make you murder someone you love so dearly.

15

I used to see several individuals walking all night and day, traveling far and near to get a quick fix. A "quick fix" means they get just enough crack cocaine to get them by until the next time they can get their hands on some money. The crack cocaine had those individuals walking through the neighborhood like zombies.

I have seen several individuals lose their families, jobs, respect, and go to prison for drugs while growing up in the South. The sad part about this is that I lived in a small, segregated town with a black majority where racism was relevant. Decreasing productivity in African American culture was natural. I saw us destroying each other with no effort, by selling poison (crack cocaine) to one another.

Crack cocaine was a way of producing genocide and homicide within our culture to keep us in a fixed mindset of being in a revolving cycle of poverty.

Powerful drugs are always on the rise to destroy a person's mind. Drugs do not care what race, culture, or religion you represent; they are known to steal your soul. Once your mind is unstable, it is hard for anyone to function in their full capacity.

On a rainy, stormy Saturday morning, I was in my grandmother's living room. My cousin Chris's friend, named Damion, came in the living room with some cocaine. Damion was about 6'2" and weighed about 210 pounds. He was 23 years old and everyone was afraid of him. He said, "Young Blood, I got something to make your teeth numb and get you high."

I said, "What you are talking about?" He stated it was that white girl in his pocket. I was young and curious, so I asked to see the cocaine. He showed it to me and told me to taste it.

He said it wouldn't do anything but numb my mouth. I agreed to taste the cocaine. As he was putting it on the table to cut it up, something told me to say no. As a matter of fact, Reese killing his grandmother told me to say NO. Damion was using his license to separate the cocaine on the glass table. The more I observed him separating the cocaine, the more my mind was saying no. I looked at Damion and remember saying, "I do not want it—and do not ask me again!"

He said, "Young Blood, you going to hit this cocaine."

I told that dude, "No disrespect, and I do not want any problems, but if you ask me again, I am going to tell my brothers."

Then, he smiled and shook his head, saying, "Okay, Young Blood, you won," and he walked out the room. Thinking about it, that was one of the best decisions I made in my life—to just say NO. My spirit always let me know when something is not in line with God. Honestly, I had to pay attention to the silent voice of God that spoke volumes through my

spirit that day.

Facts on Drugs

Research shows that drug abuse is a direct correlation to brain abnormalities (Ersche et al., 2012; Nestler, 2001). Substantial evidence shows that drug addiction is not a commodity that can be "Rehabilitated" by a duration of incapacitation (prison). The use of cocaine and heroin has been around as long as the 1890s (Musto). The majority of people in my community went to jail for selling crack, but they really were users, too.

I noticed some individuals who went to prison for as little as three small crack rocks…they had them to use, not to sell. Those individuals did prison time, but once they were free, they reverted back to the hard-core drugs that they were using before they went to prison. History shows that drug trafficking will continue as long Americans continue to purchase drugs. Therefore, we, as people, should govern our communities to decrease the war on drugs.

Dealing with Altercations

As a young man growing up, I used to sit on the grimy porch

talking all day with my partners conveying what we wanted to be when

we grew up. The answers were always the same: an ambitious drug

dealer, an adventurous basketball player, an energetic football player,

and an appealing rapper. As a young man, I was still weird. In the sixth

grade, I practiced signing my name on a piece of paper every day, saying

I was going to be famous. I also prayed every day to advance to the

next grade, however I failed that year and disgraced myself. I had

learned two things in the sixth grade. The first thing I received from that memorable year was learning that if I pray, I also have to work. The second valuable piece of information I gained was in the form of a poem that hung on the wall. The poem was about a wise old owl.

The Poem

"A wise old owl sat in an oak
The more he saw, the less he spoke
The less he spoke, the more he heard.
Why aren't we all like that wise old bird?"
(Columbian, p. A.6)

The author of the poem was unknown. However, I learned the importance of listening from that great nursery rhyme that year. I never forgot the episode of failing the sixth grade, with little changes.

Underestimating the Opposition

One chilly night I was with my homeboys Brian and Ted. We were coming from a Halloween party and were rapping the Beastie Boys song "Fight for your Right." These two young men, named Mark and Dexter, kept following us. Mark and Dexter were three years older than we were, and they had broken someone's leg with a sizeable skinny pole a week earlier.

I guess, they thought I was their next victim. I knew they wanted to fight me because I had brutally beaten their friend John up a week earlier, so I'd kept some brass knuckles in my pocket. I was dilatory as I turned and asked, "Why are you dudes following us?"

Dexter said, "I was following you because you said something to my partner named John."

I told him, "This is ridiculous ... and John's fight does not have anything to do with you." I warned Dexter to leave me alone at least three times. Dexter kept trying to hit me with a sizeable skinny pole, and I continuously avoided him. I pulled out the brass knuckles and put them on my fist.

Dexter looked at Ted and said, "Give me the brass knuckles." I guess Ted was a part of the plot to jump me, but I never found out.

Ted rushed towards me with anger in his eyes, reaching for the brass knuckles. Suddenly, I snatched my hand back and stared at him with an uncompromising frown. Dexter was gazing at the window of the store with his back turned in the opposite direction from me.

I navigated my way to Dexter slowly and tapped him on his shoulder and then punched him in his eye with the brass knuckles. I was only 13 years old at that time. He underestimated my kindness for weakness. Dexter grabbed his eye, and Mark shouted, "D**n! You busted my boy eye wide-open! It's on now!"

Mark and his partners put Dexter in the car and rushed him to the hospital. I heard police sirens and saw flashing blue and red lights. I jumped into someone's car trying to escape the nasty scene, but I did not know how to drive. I pushed the accelerator, but the car did not move. I did not think you had to put the car in drive. I jumped out of the vehicle.

After that, Brian and I found several short cuts and walked home that night. Ted went the opposite direction because he knew I was furious at him for trying to give Dexter my brass knuckles. I never talked to Ted after that night. Brian and I became best friends that nasty night.

Once I got home, I woke up Big Ma and told her exactly what had happened. Big Ma said, "I know you, Precious, and if you hit him in the eye, he had to provoke you." She said, "I am going to send you back to Chicago tomorrow morning because you are fighting too much in Mississippi."

I told my grandmother, "I did not have any cruel, defamatory intention to hurt anybody. I was only defending myself."

I learned several pointers that hot, cloudy night. I learned that when people have manipulative, cunning, deceitful, scheming, cruel, and malicious intent, they will always lose the battle. I discovered that when people think they have the advantage, sometimes they won't stop until something drastic and nasty happens to them. I also grasped the idea that I should never take anyone's kindness for weakness or underestimate anyone, because the tables can turn within seconds.

Summary (Expression): Seeking the Wrong Attention

It is easy to seek the wrong attention. Let's glance at the social learning theory for a moment. Social learning theory demonstrates how we learn from observation, which is our environmental factors. For example, we learn from our view and adapt to the surroundings of our environment. If you grew up in poverty, the only people you saw were drug dealers and factory workers. Once that individual gets older without any exposure, he thinks this is the only way to survive. This concept of survival becomes retention in the household and in the community. It becomes an ongoing cycle. Another example: if your parents and siblings are aggressive and you see this 24/7 from the time you are born until the time you become a teenager; the social learning theory expresses that you will become aggressive in comparison to your environment.

CHAPTER 2

WELCOME TO THE JUNGLE

The word "jungle" conveys distinctions, uncultivated and uncontainable nature and segregation from civilization. The jungle has emotions that evoke intimidation, misperception, powerlessness, uncertainty, and restriction. Chicago was like a jungle once I moved back. We dressed differently and did not adapt socially to the American culture. We were rebellious and isolated to our communities. Our emotions induced extortion, confusion, doubt, and limitation—which equal imprisonment and murdering. By killing and murdering over drugs and gang violence, it produces a strong sense of genocide in our black poverty-stricken communities. As people, we have to learn and understand that we are exterminating and annihilating our people by subjecting ourselves to the violence in our communities.

During this time of my life, Big Ma put me on the first train back to Chicago to live with my mother the day after I hit Dexter in the eye. While on the train, the train workers accused me of being a runaway and threatened to put me off the train. Nevertheless, they finally contacted my mother, and she acknowledged to them that I was coming to Chicago to live with her.

Once I got to Chicago, my father picked me up from the train station. We stopped at Taco Bell and got something to eat. While we

23

were eating those tasty tacos, my father conveyed to me, "You know your mother is not going to deal with all your fighting and inappropriate language you use."

I stared at him and said, "Yes, Sir," and returned to eating.

I was unable to get into school for what seemed like a massive month. My father took off of work and walked me to a new school around the corner in the five-inch-deep snow. Not to mention, I was 14 in the seventh grade. The classes were much more advanced than the ones I had taken in Lexington. I had to work and study much harder than I had studied in Mississippi.

My second day of school, it was a cold and windy, snowy day. The young men wore their hats turned to the left or the right, representing two of the furious gangs in Chicago. They watched me, and I observed them like I was a watchdog ready to attack. I was in my classroom looking outside the window, and there was white snow everywhere.

I was alone, with no friends, trying to adjust to my new environment. I knew that I was not going to do anything to fit in with the popular youth, so I always learned to stay quiet and mind my own business. Eventually, the other students started talking to me and calling me "Mississippi." When a teacher asked me a question, I always answered with "Yes, Ma'am … no, Ma'am … yes, Sir … no, Sir…"

Harry was one of my classmates when I was in the seventh grade. Harry was one smooth cat. He already had two babies by the time he was in the seventh grade. He was much more advanced than I was in life.

When I said, "Yes, Ma'am," to my teachers, Harry said, "No, no, Mississippi! "You do not say 'yes, Ma'am' around here or speak to everyone you see." He also said, "People will take your kindness for weakness and eat you up alive."

I said, "So I need to chill with all the 'yes, Ma'am' and not be friendly?"

Harry said, "Yes, Mississippi … and be careful what neighborhood you go into because they will jump you just because they do not know you." I told him I understood.

The next stormy day, I went to the suspicious corner store. I saw pimps on one corner, drug dealers on another corner, and the gang bangers fighting throughout the neighborhood.

Also, there were undercover cops driving around searching for young teens. Some young men I knew who lived in the same brown building I lived in were walking down the street talking about the new Jordan's that had just come out.

Remember, I was about 14 at this time. The police jumped out of their car and said, "Butterfly! Butterfly!"

My friend struck me on the shoulder and said, "'Butterfly' means to put your hands up." The police slammed me on the car and searched me from my head to toe. The police also searched my friends who were with me.

One cop stared at me and said, "I am going to be the patrol officer at Sinn High School next year, and I am going to make sure your life will become a living Hell."

I was thinking again, "Why do these cops keep bothering me?" I ran home as fast as I could and told my mother what had happened.

My mother went on and on talking about the scornful streets and the police. She screamed, "I told you, you have two groups of people to deal with in Chicago—the police and the gangs!"

Later that night, I went outside with my partners, who lived in the same building I lived in. I said, "Let's go to Sunny Side and Hassell where the Vice Lords hang out." As we were walking around the corner, I heard extremely loud gunshots.

I felt like I was dodging bullets from vicious hunters in the wild jungle. Individuals getting shot was normal, and individuals not getting shot was abnormal. Everything was backwards. I went upstairs one night, and my mother said, "Go to the store and get me some sweet sugar from J.J. Peppers' store." She sent 10 delightful dollars' worth of food stamps with me.

I got so upset when my mother sent me to the store with those food stamps, but I had to close my mouth and be obedient. I had two problems. I was embarrassed because my mother kept sending me to the store with those flaky food stamps and I always used to think that if someone saw me, they would laugh.

Although this was true, my mother did not understand or know that I was getting chased every time I went to a convenience store. If she wanted sugar, I had to get it.

The second problem was, for me to go to J.J. Peppers' convenience store, I had to walk past the gangsters in my neighborhood. One hot humid night during the summer of 1988, I was walking in the neighborhood and I saw a group of young men. They started running from five different directions towards me. They were shouting, "He is a Hook, and he lives over there by Sunny Side and Hassell. Let's get him!"

I had to run to the store … and pray each time I went to the store. On the way back to the house, I started out strolling, trying to sneak past them. It only took one young man to say, "There he goes! Let's get that Hook!"

I started running like I was a track star. I made it home safely that day, breathing hard and extremely fast. The next day, I was walking to the store minding my business when I saw this young man named Larry, who lived in my building. He was with five more young men.

As I was walking, I noticed the five young men had an angry disfigured facial expression with spiteful rage in their eyes. They started saying, "Vice Lord!" and "Gangster Disciple!" and were staring at me up and down. They also started throwing gang signs. I was not scared but confused.

I was thinking to myself that they were representing two different gangs … but for what reason? I said to myself "They must have lost their minds."

It was difficult for me to understand their purpose of saying, "Vice Lord! Gangster Disciple!" and throwing up gang signs. I was not a part of a gang during that time. However, they finally left, and Larry stayed with me. Thinking back on that day, I see that a person would have to have strong mental strength to make it out of my community. (My role-models were pimps and gang members, by default. I thank God for the transition—now, my role-model is Jesus and the Will of God.)

Larry was about 13, and I had just turned 15. Larry said, "They were about to take your shoes because they thought you were in a gang."

I shouted, "What?"

He said, "Yes, I told them if they were trying to take your Jordan shoes, they would have to take my shoes as well." He looked at me and said, "They do not want any problems with me, I promise!" He then asked me to walk to the store, and we became best friends that day.

As we were walking to the store, I thought, "This young man is only 13 years old and not afraid of anyone." Later that day, I went home and called my cousin, named Squeaky, who was in a gang from the West Side of Chicago.

When he answered the phone, he said, "What up, Li-cousin?"

I said, "There were some young men in my neighborhood talking about taking my shoes."

He said, "I am on my way!" and slammed down the phone.

Once he arrived, Squeaky said, "Get up, Precious, so we can go to the park now! I call the shots, and this won't happen again." On the way to the park, my cousin Squeaky said, "No one from this set will bother you again."

Then, I asked, "Why do you say that?"

He said, "I came by myself to show no fear or intimidation." He also stated, "I have respectful rank on the West Side of Chicago, and no one should bother you, or they will have problems." Once we got to the park, Squeaky went up to one of the gang members and shook his hand.

After that, Squeaky, said in a loud voice, "No one says anything to my cousin; he just moved out here from Mississippi, and he does not claim any set!" Soon after that, I started hanging out with that organization and eventually joined.

In my crime infested culture, I realized you could find yourself in three categories: Vice Lord, Gangster, or an Outcast. No one wanted to be an outcast, so as a young teenager, I was forced to decide who I was going to affiliate myself with in Chicago. As a member of one of the brutal gangs in Chicago, I had a weekly meeting, paid dues, talked with the other members every day, and hung out with them all night. I felt they were like my real brothers.

Think about it; there were so many African American men without fathers and mothers, who were left to raise themselves in a hostile, murder-infested environment and had no real guidance. They joined a gang to fill that missing piece.

Perception as a Teenager

My perceptions of the World's size and shape remain constant because of the poverty mindset I grew up in for a long time. Growing up, my perception of the World was like a flowing river with no edge. I lost myself in a world that only demonstrated manipulation, racism, hate, drugs, homeless people, and gang violence. I perceived the World as a trapped environment.

I didn't know anything different. My perception of the World was easily triggered to organize, identify, and make sense of the external behaviors in my situations. Basically, as a young man, my viewpoint of the World, became a part of my identity.

Pain from Gang Violence

Time progressed and, three years later, a young man named Vick, who worked with me, stated that his friend had been maliciously murdered. I looked at him and shook my tiny head and kept on working. Two weeks later, I heard some loud, grimy gunshots in my neighborhood at night.

I got up the next morning and brushed my tasty teeth. I rushed out of the door exceedingly fast and got on the nasty elevator, but something did not feel right. I was rushing, and the Security Guard, named Jeff, looked at me with a gigantic frown for about 5 seconds while shaking his head. Then he said, "Larry, your friend that live on the 10th floor, got shot last night."

I looked at Jeff with a smile and said, "I will go see him when I get off work."

Jeff replied, "He is unconscious and on life support." I went to work miserable and hurting, walking ten blocks to my job at a place called "The Breakers," where I tediously cleaned off tables while working with older adults who lived in that particular community.

Vick walked in the dreadful bathroom at work really slowly while brushing his hair. I was on the floor crying with tears of anger. Vick looked down at me and shook his head. He asked me, "Why are you on the floor, crying?"

I replied, "Larry was shot last night and is unconscious in the hospital."

He brought back to my attention, "Do you remember when I told you that my friend was murder two weeks ago?"

I replied, "Yes." Vick explained that I'd intentionally ignored him and said it felt different to me when it was my friend that was hurt. At a young age, I learned empathy. Under those circumstances, you never know how it feels unless you put yourself in someone else's shoes.

I got off the floor and asked my manager, "Can I go see Larry at the hospital?"

My manager said, "Sure ... and sorry about your friend.

Dealing with Hurt

I went to the hospital where gang members, family members, and close friends were standing around in a state of shock. I went into the remorseful room, and Larry's mother was sitting beside the bed. That was her only son.

My partner, Larry, was on life support, and it changed my thought process extremely fast seeing my close friend in a helpless situation. The next day, they pulled him off life-support. After Larry's funeral, I stayed in my room for weeks praying, tossing, and turning.

My mother slowly opened the door in my room each day, shouting, "You do not own those streets!" She also screamed extremely loudly, "Martin Luther King and Medgar Evers died for us to be free! You can go to school and get a job or stay in the street and go to jail or prison!"

Then, she decreased her voice tone, saying, "There is a right road and a bad road. You can pick your choice," and she slammed the door.

My mother was ruthless at that memorable moment. My mother showed me tough love because she did not want me to be another victim of teenage gang violence in our stumbling society.

Her strategy worked, and I carried those words in my heart and mind. Until this day, those words my mother had spoken are in my spirit. Those words changed my behavior. A couple of months later, my mother sent me back to Mississippi to live with Big Ma. My mother preached the significance of being free to remind me to recover myself as a man when faced with adversity.

Summary (Expression): Welcome to the Jungle

Our culture shapes and customizes our identity. If we are restricted within a social environment stipulated by our culture, we will slightly be regulated from the rest of the world. For example, if you have never seen anyone studying, reading, or writing, you will not know that reading and writing will enhance your conscious awareness. Being deprived of experience or exposure, we become culture-bound. Several nonconformists do not transpire because they are not known to our culture. I was a victim of not studying, using profanity, and conforming to the filthy street life because it was a way of life in my culture. I never held a conversation with a person of a different race or a professional, like a lawyer or a doctor, until I went to college.

CHAPTER 3

PERCEPTION

Deep Insight

Our perception demonstrates how we identify mechanisms: cognitive and neural. Our cognition is our conscious intellectual gathering of information. Cognition is how we entail knowledge and gather information, which assists us with navigating the information through our mind.

After Larry was murdered, I moved back to Lexington, Mississippi with a population of 1,500 people. I did my best to try to stop gang banging. However, I could not shake the stunning street life. I became more enticed to the stupendous streets in Lexington by bringing all the gang literature to Mississippi. I have been known as the young man who brought gangs to a small town with a population of 1,500 people. The same cycle from Chicago transferred to Lexington, Mississippi.

I had a cousin named Cle who was a part of the crew. We used to hang out from sun-up until sun-down daily. Cle was about six feet tall with a high-top fade and was always brushing his hair. Cle's father was the leader of a gospel singing group. Cle played the drums in the singing group.

His father had a song called, "Don't Let them Shake my Faith." I used to listen to that song every time I went into Cle's house. Cle always had good in him, but he enjoyed the street life, too.

One cloudy night, Cle and I took a ride to Durant, Mississippi truck stop where our crew used to hang out. While Cle and I were outside talking in the parking lot, we heard a loud gunshot fired. POW! Suddenly, people started ducking, running, screaming, and crying. Big Don, another member of my crew, had been shot in the head and was pronounced dead on site.

I was shaking my head. I had lost another partner to the senseless, violent gang crimes. I evaluated my life and realized that I did not want to become another statistic. Indeed, gang violence kept happening in Holmes County.

One night I was on my knees praying for God to take that reputation off of me ... I did not know Big Ma was listening. When I opened my eyes, Big Ma was looking at me. She smiled at me and said,

"Son, God heard your prayers."

Praying

"And when you pray, do not be like the hypocrites, for they love to pray standing in the synagogues and on the street corners to be seen by others. Truly I tell you, they have received their reward in full. But when you pray, go into your room, close the door and pray to your Father, who is unseen. Then your Father, who sees what is done in secret, will reward you. And when you pray, do not keep on babbling like pagans, for they think they will be heard because of their many words. Do not be like them, for your Father knows what you need before you ask him." (New International Version, Mathew 6:5-15)

Shooting at School

I had a homeboy named Sly who was a church-going young man. Sly went to school in Durant, Mississippi, but lived in Lexington. Sly's grandmother worked for the board of education and she was a devoted teacher. Sly was one of the young men that didn't get involved with gangs, and he came from a prestigious family. Sly's family used to ask me, "What college are you going to attend next year?"

I had no earthly idea about going to college. The only thing I wanted to do was hang out with my homeboys and spend time with my gorgeous lady friends. I did not think I was even smart enough to go to college. Sly was 16 years old and driving a new Honda Accord. I thought he was rich. His parents used to go to Hawaii all the time.

I also had a friend named Marcus, and he was a part of the crew I hung out with in my neglected neighborhood. Marcus was a close partner and we hung out like brothers.

One stormy night, Marcus, Sly and I were riding down the street. We were in route to my ex-girlfriend Tiffany's house. I told Sly not to stop, but he continued and stopped the smooth clean Honda accord car in front of her house. Once he stopped, Tiffany's new boyfriend, Tod, came out of the house.

Tod was upset with me because my ex-girlfriend and I had exchanged words at school. Tod started walking towards me extremely fast with aggression. When he got close to me, I hit him.

Tod threw me. As I was falling to the ground, I was punching him as fast as I could. Once we hit the ground, my friend Marcus started punching him with uncontrollable rage. We got up and Tod started approaching me swiftly with irritated wrath.

I punched Tod again and Marcus hit him with a battered broom. Sly and Tiffany broke the fist fight up. Tod pointed at Marcus with a mugging face, saying, "I am going to freaking kill you, Marcus." We jumped into Sly's brown getaway car and fled the scene.

After that, Marcus got frustrated. Marcus started shooting his gun in the air near the woods. He started saying, "I am from hard-core Jackson, Mississippi and he threatened my life; I got to have him on Monday!"

Marcus also said, "You will see me on the news Monday the next time I see him because he has threatened my life."

Honestly, I thought he was just talking in general. Monday morning, I was walking down the long narrow hallway at school, and all I heard was a gunshot. Pow! Students were running and screaming in every direction. This girl bumped me and said, "Tod shot Marcus!"

I asked, "What?"

She shouted, "NO! Marcus shot Tod and the police got Marcus in custody at the principal's office!" The officers transported Marcus to the police station. My crew and I went to the station to see Marcus.

I asked Marcus what happened. Marcus said, "He threatened me Friday night, and I had to protect myself." Marcus' whole career was gone with the blink of an eye. Tod was in intensive care for about a month, and Marcus did about a year in the county jail for the school shooting.

I was feeling so bad behind that situation, because Marcus was helping me fight and ended up shooting a good person. I prayed to God for forgiveness. I just needed something to get me out that lifestyle.

One warm, windy night, I went to a dance at Jacob J. McClain High School. A girl named Tiffany was sitting on the bleachers flirting with me and saying that she wanted me to be her boyfriend. I told her I would think about it because I already had someone that I was interested in having as a girlfriend.

She went on to say she did not care and grabbed my head and started kissing me. I was shocked, but I kissed her back. Out of nowhere, this dude named Billy D. walked up to us with two of his partners. He said, "Why are you kissing my girl?"

I said, "You do not know me partner and this is not what you want." While this young man was talking to me, he did not know that all my homeboys were standing around him.

Kelly was a part of my crew and he did not back down from anyone. Kelly saw the whole situation transpire but stayed quiet. He eased behind one of the young men who said something to me and punched him in the face.

I punched his homeboy and my crew came from every different direction headed to the fight until the security guards broke it up. We all left, and Kelly asked me to follow him to the car. He pulled out a gun and got on one knee waiting on Billy's car to pass.

Kelly had his hand on the trigger; he shot one time and missed. I looked at him and said, "This is not worth it Bro'; put the gun up and let's get out of here." I went to Brian's house that night and we talked about what had happened. Brian, who was a part of our crew, became my new partner whom I hung out with daily and we developed a brotherly bond. Brian and I were similar, but different.

Brian was very reserved, but no one bothered him because they knew he was quiet and was not afraid of anyone. I conveyed to Brian that it seemed like trouble is drawn to me like a magnet. I told Brian I did not even know that young lady and she kissed me. Brian said, "How was the kiss?"

I remember laughing it off like, "Bro' someone almost got shot and you asking me about a kiss?"

Brian said, "Listen Bro', this altercation started over a kiss from a female you did not know. I just wanted to know if the kiss was worth us going to jail or someone getting shot?"

I looked at him and stated, "I think we were at the wrong place at the wrong time."

Brian said, "Exactly." Brian made it clear to me that I was a natural-born leader. He stated that people followed me because they believed in me. He also stated that I have to be careful of how I move and think so that no one gets hurt in our crew. I drank some Kool-Aid and gave him some dap before I left his house. That was some really good advice that I needed to hear.

For months after that night I tried to escape the street life; however, the problems just kept coming … more women, more problems!

In 1992, my homeboy Kelly went to prison for murder. Kelly ended up receiving a life sentence for a murder in Durant, Mississippi. The organization in Lexington steadily grew more and more. I was praying and feeling the pain of different families losing loved ones.

My brother Johnny stepped up and said he would be the leader of the gang to protect me. He was trying to save me, and I did not know it. They voted and Johnny instantly became the man. Wow! Johnny was so wise that he joined the gang to make a peace treaty across Holmes County just to cease the senseless murders.

Johnny held a meeting with all the gangs in the county and we all voted on a peace treaty. It was a sensational sight to see. Individuals who had been shooting at and fighting with each other met up for the same cause. Things had been going smoothly since the peace treaty.

However, one night my cousin Terrence got drunk at this club called the "Yellow Tree" and started throwing up gang signs. Instantly, a war broke out with guns and shootings. My friend Richard was murdered at the Yellow Tree that night. He was about 6'4" and weighed about 225 pounds. He was good friend.

Lord, have mercy! I was in a place of confusion, guilt, and pain. Richard's murder case has not been solved to this day. Johnny was extremely hurt when Richard was murdered.

Johnny had amended the peace treaty to stop the senseless murders, but one individual drinking with no restraints after two months of no violence caused a tragic death. That tragic murder caused a youthful war in my community. Eventually, Johnny stepped down after the peace treaty had been broken. After Johnny stepped down, the fighting and shooting reached their maximization because everyone wanted revenge.

With that in mind, I shot basketball daily to remove myself from the street life. In school, I was only an average student with no earthly idea of what I was going to do. I knew staying in Lexington was not an option. During all the confusion, Sly asked me to go to college and suggested I sign up to take the ACT. I did not understand anything about the ACT or testing to get into college. Nevertheless, I wanted to see something different. I needed a different atmosphere.

Once we went to Jackson State University to take the ACT, I noticed young men and women being happy and having fun. They were sitting on the lawn on campus, reading and writing. I said, "This place is where I want to reside after high school." I saw young people socializing cheerfully without hurting one another.

Summary (Expression): Perception

Each stage of my life demonstrated a cognitive process that occurred outside of my conscious awareness and influenced my conscious perception and cognition. For instance, getting out my community one day with a friend who lived in a more stable and prestigious environment enhanced my conscious awareness to see something different and want something different. Our conscious illustration of what we have recognized in our so-called World often changes tremendously to non-conscious once we are exposed to something different. Once we are exposed to something different, we can modify and alter our thought process by transferring our negative mindset to a positive mindset. We sometimes see people who never change; those individuals who do not change usually stay in a constant perception mindset. Often, when a person remains in a consistent mindset, they have what you call a "tunnel vision." They only see things one way and are not open to change.

CHAPTER 4
SELF-DISCIPLINE: ALWAYS PREPARED

Self-discipline is a sharp instrument to use. Self-discipline represents the ability to restrain and control oneself. Emotions are a part of our instinct that provokes our behavior, whether if it is impulsive or unconscious. As individuals, we must discipline our emotions by controlling our core feelings by recognizing the signs of frustration. We must understand our discomfort moods. Once we identify those uneasy feelings of stress that activate our emotions, we must develop an exit plan.

When I graduated from high school, I decided to change my life. I had to learn favorable discipline fast. I never made the honor roll in high school and I never studied in school, either. I thought everyone around me was brilliant.

During the summer of 1992, I received a letter stating that I was accepted to a local college near Jackson, Mississippi. I was overwhelmed and happy to get an opportunity to change my life and mindset.

I went and told one of my cousins that I was going to college. My cousin Faye and her friends looked at me and started laughing. Faye said, "You not going to do anything but drop out like everyone else." She also said, "You will not make it in college—go get a job!" Then, she laughed extremely loudly at me.

At this point, I felt like the lowest person on Earth. Here it is, the best day of my life, and it went sour with several negative comments. I went into the back room and was filled with frustration, doubting myself.

My father came into the room and sat down next to me. He said, "I heard everything they said about you. You cannot listen to the words they are saying in the next room, and they are not talking in their right minds at this moment."

He continued to explain by telling me he had gone to college, but did not graduate because at that time, schools did not have Pell Grants. "Go to school and do your best. If you drop out, you still did more than a lot of other students."

After that, my father looked me directly in my eyes with a tear coming down the right side of his face, saying, "You can do whatever you want to do in life, my son. You will do very well."

After that day, my confidence level went sky-high. I felt I could move a mountain. I also thought that I could be successful. I went to college in the summer of 1992. When school started, my life changed … and so did my friends in my community from Lexington.

I had a friend named Joe from my hometown who stayed in my room for a whole year. He sold drugs in the nearby community in Jackson. I used to walk in my room from class and drugs were all over the bed and floor. My room was full of drug dealers and young men shooting dice.

All I saw were the twenties and fives. The music was so loud that I could not study or concentrate. Everyone always had a cup in their hand. The only thing going through my mind was that I came here for an education and not to hang out. It got so bad. I had no control over my life or my room.

The same cycle from the hood had transferred to college. I had to look at the common denominator, which pointed directly to me. I had to accept that street life gravitated to me wherever I went. The street life had shifted from Chicago to Lexington to college.

One weekend, I left college and went to Lexington to visit the Yellow Tree. I was at the club having a blast when suddenly, my homeboy named Clay pushed me for no reason. I turned around and stared at him and said, "What up?"

He continued, "You looked at my girlfriend." Clay and I were a part of the same crew. My first thought was to punch him, and my second thought was to tell my brother Johnny. I knew that if I had punched him and Johnny had been in the club, someone would have gotten hurt really badly. Instead, I was steadfast and thought about the negative consequences.

I went back to school and prayed to God to forgive Clay and allow him to apologize to me. The next weekend, Clay came and apologized. He also treated me to a meal. God showed me that day if we let Him fight our battles and pray for salvation and forgiveness for our enemies, He will provide (Jehovah Jireh).

I had a role model named Curtis. Curtis is my oldest cousin. I looked up to Curtis for guidance. He was like a brother and father to me. He went to the same college, as well.

He was structured. He served in the military and was always willing to help. Curtis' crew, which included Marzette and Coop, was small, but they were always reliable. Marzette, and Coop always gave me good advice and they were always willing to help guide me in the right direction.

Curtis told me that I had to withdraw from school to keep my GPA from dropping. I took my cousin's advice and withdrew from school at the end of my first college school year. Now, Joe had left and gone home about a week before school got out. That gave my cousin Curtis and his crew some time to speak some sense into my head.

My cousin called me to his room and said, "You are street smart and thorough with gang knowledge." He also stated, "If you brought gangs from Chicago to Lexington and had individuals to follow you, Cousin, you do not understand the strength you have within yourself."

I said, "Why you say that? I am not that smart, Cousin."

Curtis looked at me and shook his head with a smile. Then he spoke slowly and said, "You could take all that negative energy and turn it into positive." He elaborated, "Little Cousin, if you can turn your street sense into book sense, your strength will be beyond your measure."

I said, "What? Are you serious?"

He said, "Yes, if you can learn gang literature, you can learn your school work with no problems." I took my cousin's advice and withdrew from school. I went home two weeks before school got out.

While at home waiting for the summer break to start, I went uptown to get a juice and some potato logs at Jitney Junior's convenient store. I saw Joe at the Jitney Junior's and he asked me "Why you're not in school?"

I replied, "I withdrew from college just for this one semester."

He looked at me with a sneaky smile and told me, "I knew you were going to drop out." Wow. I stopped and looked at him. Then, I shook my head and walked off. The only thing that was going through my mind was that he was in my room the whole year distracting me from my destiny and I let him.

After that day, I called my father and told him, "I need two-thousand dollars to get back in to school."

My father replied, "Son, I will pay this fee for you, but you have to remember that I will not do this again. Therefore, my son, you need to finish the process."

I went back to school with the mindset of self-control and self-discipline. Every morning, I got up and I worked out. I also went to the library every night at 6:00 pm. I started watching my eating habits daily. I made up in my mind that I was not drinking any more alcohol and I was going to focus on school. I actually had to get back to the basics and was on-track with my grades.

I had to go back and study second- and third-grade English books because I did not pay attention in class when I was younger. I used to stay at the University library every night from six until the library closed. One night around nine, one of my classmates saw me in the library studying for a test. She laughed and asked, "You have been in here studying for the same test since earlier today?"

I replied, "Yes."

She said, "It did not take me but an hour to study for that easy English exam." I smiled and returned to my studying. I stayed consistent with studying and learning the basic tools I needed to advance in college and in life. Instead of being embarrassed, I took a negative situation and completely did a transformation to change my academic situation. That year was the beginning of me making the honor roll until I graduated.

Paradigm Shift

During this time, my girlfriend at that moment was pregnant with my daughter, so I felt I had to make a drastic change in my life to take care of my daughter. I decided to change my thought process entirely from negative to positive, which was a result of that paradigm shift.

I decided that the gang life I had once lived would be my tool to reach young men. I wanted to encourage them to think positively, to strive to improve their life situations, and understand that their circumstance is not always their reality.

Years earlier, I had such a bad reputation that my friends' mothers did not want me in their homes. They felt that I was a bad influence on their children, which was true at the time. However, people were looking at the surface. God was looking at what he had created within me. I prayed every night to be a better person in life and to take that negative reputation off myself.

God answered my prayers. My friends' parents became the most influential and supportive people in my life. They came to my college graduations and became extra mothers, with insight to support my aspirations and encourage me to see things differently.

Summary (Expression): Self-Discipline: Always Prepared

Wolves continuously guard and mark their home turf with their scent-mark. Howling also demonstrates territorial limitations. The wolves howl to the moon to mark their area for control. The moon does not move when the wolf is howling. Silence is exceptionally significant in self-control. The moon never responds to the wolf. To destroy all anxiety in my life, I had to thoroughly annihilate, exterminate, and liquidate any task that caused any frustration, confusion or hindering situation that restrained me from my goals.

CHAPTER 5
THIRD EYE: BEING OBJECTIVE

The pineal gland is what we call the "Third Eye." The focal point of our Third Eye is the pineal gland. The Third Eye is a natural part of every individual. As you read below, this chapter will give you more insight and understanding of the Third Eye.

It was the first month of school during the 1993 Fall Semester. I had a homeboy named Kenny. Kenny and I were contemplating on going to Lexington one night to visit our parents.

Kenny was a very educated young man who attended Jackson State University with me. I was a Sophomore, and Kenny was a Freshman. Kenny lived in the projects where shooting, fighting, and gang activities were a consistent way of life. Although he lived in the vicious gang community that I fought against in high school, he did not partake in any gang activities.

Once we got to Lexington, we decided to stop by my friend Timothy's house before we visited our parents. He was excited that we stopped by his house. Timothy was my funny, cool partner. He did not smoke or drink any alcohol. Timothy was always alert and paid close attention to details. Timothy asked me to trade cars that night because he needed to run a couple of errands.

I agreed to swap cars and Kenny and I drove around town listening to Michael Jackson's song "Billy Jean." Timothy's car had 10-inch speakers that were extremely loud and heavy. The song "Billy Jean" was so loud that our ears were ringing. You could hear Michael Jackson two miles away!

As we were riding, we noticed that a car started following us slowly. Kenny turned around and said, "They from my hood."

I said, "What?" We decided to pull up at the Double-Quick store around some lights and the car pulled up right beside us. Inside there were four young men staring at us with bloodshot red eyes and guns in the car. They looked like they were on an evil mission. Even worse, all four of the young men who were in the car were part of the opposing gang to the one that I had affiliated myself with before I went to college.

Craig, the passenger in the car that had been following us, yelled at Kenny, saying, "You got a problem with me?" Quickly, my mind started to race. As my mind was circulating, I realized they had a problem with me and not Kenny.

I stared at them without fear and said, "If you got a problem with me, then say it."

Craig said, "As a matter of fact, I do have a problem with you." He then reached down between his seat and showed me his black and gray nine-millimeter gun.

I said, "I am not participating in any gang activities anymore."

At that moment, Craig's face disfigured with a rage as he replied, "No, you still banging unless we say it is over." I had an absence of thoughts at that very second and I drove off to my house with revenge on my mind. While I was driving, they tailed my car to the house.

As soon as I got home, I went into the house and picked up the phone and called my big brother, Johnny. Johnny listened to me and said, "Put Kenny on the phone." Johnny asked Kenny what had happened, and Kenny told Johnny the same solid story I had conveyed to Johnny minutes earlier. Johnny told Kenny, "Put Precious on the phone." When I picked up the phone, Johnny said, "Stay in place until I get there tomorrow."

I called Timothy as well to let him know what had just happened. Timothy said, "I am on my way now." About 20 minutes later, Timothy pulled up with a sawed-off rifle and said, "Let's get them now."

I shook my head and told Timothy, "My brother told me not to do anything until he gets off work tomorrow."

Timothy said, "Okay. It is on tomorrow." Eventually, Timothy left and gave me the rusty rifle to keep. After that, I asked Kenny to go home because it was not his fight.

I went into the house and analyzed the whole scenario from that night. I reenacted the whole situation over and over in my mind all night long to see what had happened. Immediately, I came up with the conclusion: I had positioned myself in a dangerous lifestyle at a young age. I was still trying to modify my behavior by not being a part of that violent lifestyle anymore.

Nevertheless, there was always that one person trying to entice me to succumb to my old lifestyle. I got up the next morning and went outside to shoot some ball. On my way to the basketball court, I saw the car belonging to the young man who had been following me the night before. He was on the basketball court shooting basketball in front of my house. Now, I was thinking, "He's got some nerve — in my neighborhood and shooting ball the next day."

Suddenly, I ran into the house and grabbed the rifle. I returned and sat on top of his white car. He looked at me and started walking my way. As he was walking towards me, my heart was pumping, and my life flashed in front of me. I had my hand on the trigger.

My brother and his friends pulled up at that same moment about five cars behind us. Surprisingly, they all had guns and were ready to use them. My brother asked me, "Did that young man who was walking toward you say anything to you last night?"

I said, "He did not say anything, but they were driving his car."

My brother told me, "Get off his car and let's uncover this situation by locating Craig, the person who did say something to you." Johnny, his crew, and I jumped in different cars and drove fast. Johnny dodged a ditch and I was shaking and scared, but I had to keep my cool.

A young man named John flagged us down. He was breathing hard and fast. John said, "Timothy and Craig got into a big fight. Timothy saw Craig and jumped out the car swinging." He continued, screaming in a loud high-pitched voice, "Timothy was beating Craig up bad! The police pulled up, so Timothy and Craig went to jail!" John put the beer to his mouth and said, "All the Gangsters and Vice Lords went to jail, too."

We jumped back in the cars and headed to the police station. As I walked down the hallway, I heard screaming and yelling. The police station was packed with young gang members. Johnny was standing beside his partner Sweet.

Sweet was Johnny's right hand man and he was treacherous and ready for anything. Johnny told the police that I was not in a gang anymore or affiliated with gangs. Craig looked at my brother and said, "So Precious is the good son."

Sweet, shouted, "If anyone messes with him, I will go back to prison, and I just got out!"

The police officer said, "Let's stop this now ... and leave Precious alone."

We all parted ways and left the police station. I stayed at home with my grandmother that night because I meant what I had said about changing my life. The next morning, I was on Big Ma's porch drinking some red super-sweet Kool-Aid that my grandmother had made. My partner Vincent opened the gate and walked onto my porch, followed by Levy. Levy held his head down and started smiling with a shiny Gold tooth. He said, "Precious, the car that was following you got shot up last night." He also told me that Craig and three of his friends were in the car.

I said, "What? I am so glad I stayed at home last night." Levy started laughing with a sneaky smirk, saying that two of them got shot and that they would think twice before they said something to me again.

I remember telling Levy that I did not have anything to do with that situation. I also conveyed to Levy that I just wanted to finish college and give my daughter, Little Precious, a better life than I had growing up.

Levy expressed to me that he wanted to see me do well. He then told me that he would take care of my grandmother while I was in college. I asked him if he wanted some Kool-Aid. Levy said yes and I went into the house and grabbed him a glass of cold sweet Kool-Aid.

I gave him the Kool-Aid and told him that there was a cycle that would continue if we didn't make up our minds to change. "My best friend, Larry, was murdered in Chicago over a corner he does not own. His death was not mentioned on the news or in the Chicago Tribune—not one time," I told Levy. "Listen, Bro', once I went to college, I realized that there is a better life for us. I am going to dedicate my life to gaining knowledge and teaching these young individuals how to make it out the hood."

Levy told me, "I believe you can do it, Precious, but I am caught up in the street life. Do not forget about me when you become successful."

I said, "If I am successful, my people will be successful. We live through each other." I told Levy I had to get ready to go back to school. We gave each other a pound handshake and went our separate ways.

I went back to school with a disciplined mind. The next weekend, I went back to Lexington and I saw Craig at Jitney Jungle. I was with my mother. Craig stared at me for about five minutes but walked off rocking his head.

That same night I went home and wrote my homeboy Kelly, who had received a life sentence in prison for a murder conviction he caught in Durant, Mississippi. I mentioned to Kelly in the letter that if Craig looked at me again, I was going to hurt him, but I was doing my best to stay out of trouble. Kelly replied in his letter, "Prison is not for anybody, not even me … and you know how I was in those streets."

I thought about what he had said. He was right, I needed to focus on my baby girl, Little Precious, and focus on school. That day changed my life. Just reading the words that Kelly wrote to me assisted me with thinking before I reacted. As months passed, I stayed out of trouble and Levy kept his word and took care of my grandmother.

Levy had a case hanging over his head. My grandmother called me one day. "Precious I am so mad," she began. "Levy mows my grass, helps me around the house, and he goes to the grocery store for me."

I said, "That is good, Big Ma … and why you are mad again?"

She said, "Levy was found guilty for that case they pinned on him a year ago." She mentioned that Levy had been good help around the house, and that she hoped he would be ok. I told Big Ma that Levy would be strong while he was in prison. She said, "Okay, Precious. I am going to pray for him."

I was grateful that I had implemented my Third Eye and was seeing things differently and practicing self-discipline.

Being Objective

I customized, strategized, and organized a task while monitoring my mission and applying my plan. I had to be able to adjust when faced with any difficult situation. I used a problem-solving approach: Stop, look, listen, think and react.

I had to adjust to my atmosphere by observation and pay close attention to detail. I evaluated my life, my plans, my goals, and most of all my critical internal feelings. I criticized my behavior and approached it from a different angle. I educated myself on my eating habits. I stopped eating meat and read different books daily.

I changed my surroundings and joined an awesome fraternity, Omega Psi Phi. I learned that true brotherhood existed without fighting and hurting one another. Once I became a member of my fraternity, I graduated the same year with a 3.7 GPA from college. Who would ever think a young man from the 'hood would go to college and graduate Summa Cum Laude?

I heard of former classmates speaking on my success saying, "He graduated from college and did not do anything in high school." Little did they know that, while they were focusing on me, I was focusing on my goals.

I was playing the strategic game of chess in my everyday life by thinking two steps ahead of those individuals who were judging me, because I did not look back. I made God my foundation, and I was willing to help others with a sound mind. My process reasoning came into play when I graduated from college.

My Third Eye gave me a new perspective on life. I started observing things much differently and strategically. I started thinking about the consequences of my actions, regardless of whether they were good or bad, and that became my number one priority.

Summary (Expression): Third Eye: Being Objective

I used my Third Eye to be very crafty, which acknowledged the natural evolution that allows us substance to see the patterns in our life. Even more astonishing, your Third Eye can uncover patterns you have that superimpose information that adds to your five senses. Your Third Eye is being objective to gaze at things that we cannot see in the natural eye. Your Third Eye is being empathetic. objective and focused. Being objective is determined by not being subjected, influenced, or manipulated by personal feelings or thoughts in reflecting and representing facts.

CHAPTER 6
YOUR ACTIONS FOLLOW YOUR BELIEF

Who are You?

Who are you? I am a human being. The phenomenon of me is mine to preserve and sustain, mine to protect, mine to practice, mine to respect and mine to bow before God. I am not in oppression for the world, I am not an instrument to be mistreated, and I am not in captivity with internal forgiveness. I am a King, who is free in the mind. I will not concede to the wickedness of the world. I will be free. I am a spiritual being who God formed in His own image. I am a man of resilience. Do you know who you are? Do you know where your inheritances comes from? Yes, I do! You are genetically connected to the Great, "I am Who I am" I come, as I am; I am, as I come. I come as a man just wanting to do the will of God.

Living on the edge consists of my actions following my beliefs in this stage of my life. Around 1999, I had been out of college for two years. I graduated with my bachelor's degree in 1997, with no money, little support and barely enough money to pay my bills.

Two years later, I was still looking for a job everywhere. I always heard that if you go to college, you would be successful. Not where I am from. It was more like once you graduated from college, you would have to take a test to prove yourself, or you had to know someone in that field of work. I was sitting on the floor in a dark room and sensed that I was in a bottomless pit with no way out.

A constant thought was in my head: I had a degree with no job, money, or a place to call home. I thought about my credit and how I was not taught to manage my finances as a teenager. I closed my eyes and reminisced as a young man, thinking about how my friends used to say, "We have to get it out the mud." I did not understand what they were saying at that moment. However, as my eyes were closed, I gathered a full understanding of the true meaning of "getting it out the mud."

The mud represents a painful and malicious state of mind. As my mind went on a journey, I thought "getting it out the mud" exemplified that you had to be a person who could overcome pain, be resilient, and persevere to the end. The mud is dirty and nasty.

I felt I was dirty and dangerous growing up with ZERO chances of being successful because of the racism, poverty, and lack of exposure to positive things. During my critical thinking process, I said to myself, "I am going to get rid of all the toxic and painful generational thoughts."

My thoughts shifted into the atmosphere at that moment.

I had a constant repetitive idea that went through my mind over and over again, "There has to be a better way. I am tired of living on the edge, and my actions have to follow my beliefs." I finally opened my eyes with a new understanding of doing things differently. I jumped up, saying, "I've got to be a little wiser to get ahead and filter everything negative in my life."

I recognized that I had to turn anything in my life that looked negative to positive by any means necessary. I promised myself that I would persevere, listen before speaking, speak when spoken to, not sag, always say "yes, Ma'am" and "no, Ma'am." I told myself that I would still use "please" and "thank you," demonstrate integrity daily, learn as much as possible, and help others.

This was the game-changing moment and the beginning of my new system to fight against this internal war I was dealing with in my mind. I tossed and turned all night.

Once the morning came, I got off the floor and walked slowly towards the wall. At that moment, I cut the lights on twice: the house lights and the lights in my mind. I went to my old job at Long Star restaurant and asked my manager if I could get my old job back; I needed to work. He rehired me, and I started putting in applications everywhere. I went to the restaurant every day and still was unable to take care of my daughter and my family.

My daughter, Little Precious, was around five years old at that time. My relationship with my daughter's mother, Christine, went exceptionally well until one night when I went home and I saw an extra pair of shoes on the floor. I walked to the back, and another young man was in the house with my baby's mother, Christine.

I was broke, broken, and hurt. I left, walking with my head down and feeling sad. I did not understand why this was happening to me. I got into my car and drove from Jackson to Lexington that night—speeding extremely fast. I went to Big Ma's shotgun house. Big Ma was in her early seventies at that time.

I knocked on the door and she came to the door and opened it slowly, saying, "It is 2 a.m. and I was praying for you." She stared at me and stated, "You have tears in your eyes, and I can feel your pain. Come in and have a seat."

I told her what had happened and explained my financial situation. Big Ma sat down beside me and told me, "I love you baby and you are special." She told me that she only had her burial money, but that she would give me a thousand dollars to get out of the situation and get back on my feet. She also mentioned that she would leave me her shotgun house after she died, so I would always have somewhere to go. She explained that once she was gone, I would have to take care of myself. I kissed my sweet Big Ma and went back to Jackson.

The next day, I asked my cousin Curtis and my partner Marzette if I could move in with them until I got myself together. Coop was their partner too. Coop, Curtis, and Marzette demonstrated real mentoring and brotherly love. The three of them were in the military. They were exceedingly disciplined. Coop, Curtis, and Marzette were much older, and they gave me a lot of insight into life. Curtis talked to me about staying in shape and being disciplined daily.

While living with my cousin, I was hired at the prison. I became the youngest sergeant there in three months. Things started to expedite exceptionally fast for the best. I had a consistent daily routine for months. When I woke up, I prayed and worked out for two hours, I read the Bible for an hour, and then I prepared myself to go to work.

My work hours were from 3 p.m. to 11 p.m. When working in the prison system, I had to be on a tower watching inmates. When I went to each tower to do my counts, I did 50 pushups on each tower. The prison

I worked in was a processing and receiving facility. I saw every inmate who had been sentenced at the state level in Mississippi.

I had to face many individuals who I knew from the streets. My friends from my community expected me to compromise my character and to do illegal favorites for them. I did not jeopardize my job or who I was as a person while working in the prison system. My old peers had to respect me. I lost a few partners because they did not understand my path.

One day, I was working in the cafeteria and all the young men from the same organization I used to represent were sitting at the table making gang gestures. I told them to stop and one of the members jumped up in my face. After that, the entire table jumped up and looked at me. I was faced with at least 20 murderers and robbers who were doing at least 10 years to life.

One of them said, "I know you and I know who you are, and we know where you from." Then he said, "What's up, Sell-out?" They started walking towards me slowly.

I got nervous and looked over at the other officer, Michael, who was in the cafeteria with me. He'd just had a triple-bypass heart surgery. I knew he did not need any extra stress or to participate in any physical activity. Therefore, I had to do something swift.

I knew it was about to go down, however, I walked slowly and calmly to the window and told the control room officer to call a 1017. A "1017" radio call means all free officers from all units and the k-9 unit need to come to the response because there is an emergency.

It took them less than 5 minutes to arrive. While I was waiting on the officers, I just let them talk and I stayed quiet. Once the officers got there, they made all the inmates get on the black and white floor.

The Captain told the leader of the gang that he knew everything about Sergeant Barnett's gang-affiliated background and never to disrespect me again. He told them if any of his members said anything else to me or attempted to disrespect his Sergeant, they would get another charge for threatening an officer and would be put in supermax until they got shipped out.

Next, I had to do an incident report, and an institutional lockdown was set in motion. An institutional lockdown in prison mainly means that you are restrained to a cell for 24 hours. There were no external activities such as outside exercising, church, school, or any movement in the prison. I didn't have any more problems and they knew that my administrator knew about my street life. They could not hold my street affiliation over my head. I learned at an early age be open about your past to demonstrate trust and change.

Summary (Expression): Your Actions Follow Your Belief

The American Dream—What are our beliefs? In America, we believe that an ordinary individual, through extremely hard work and determination, will be allowed the opportunity to achieve their goals. A fundamental part of our belief is that individuals who are born in poverty can live a normal life. A normal life for individuals living in my community is abnormal to the average person. A normal life in my community is having a nice car (not owning it), making enough money to pay the bills for the month without going into the overdraft, being able to buy some Air Jordan's, and being able to put rims on our cars. My understanding of the American Dream is to own your house, own your car, own your business …having the big white picket fence, owning the dogs, and being able to send your children to college. If we know in our hearts what it takes to live the American dream, our actions must follow our beliefs.

CHAPTER 7
FORGIVENESS

"If we confess our sins, He is faithful and just and will forgive us our sins and purify us from all unrighteousness." (1 John 1:9)

Encountering a Racist Situation

My life stayed on the edge, but I knew God had something else for me to do while I was working at the prison. I stayed steadfast. I saw things that changed my outlook on life while working in Mississippi's prison system.

I met Byron De La Beckwith and Sam Bowers while working there. Beckwith was an American white supremacist. He was a Klansman from Greenwood, Mississippi who killed our great civil rights leader, Medgar Evers, on June 12, 1964. He was convicted and sentenced. A new trial displayed more evidence in 1994.

When I went into the supermax to do my count, I talked to Beckwith. I had to take him a tray. I could not believe the words that came out of his mouth in 1999. One day I was giving him his food, and he told me that he did not like "niggas." He also stated the only thing worst then a "nigga" was a "Japanese."

I looked at him and smiled. I still treated him nicely and with respect. I realized at a young age that I had to be accountable for my actions. I learned a lot from our conversations. I learned that Byron De La Beckwith was talking to an African American man with no regard for what he was saying or how he felt. He spoke to me like I was a white supremacist and did not care what he was saying.

One day I was dropping off a tray and he said, "You need to get several guns and train your family how to shoot them." He also stated that his family had several guns and knew how to use them. I was working the midnight shift at this time. After my first encounter with him, I sat in one position on the tower thinking about how he had murdered Medgar Evers.

The thought also went through my mind that it had been over thirty years ago, and he still felt the same lack of remorse. Beckwith took kindly to me. Every day he asked me about my family and how I was doing. I felt that he was indirectly telling me to teach my family how to shoot a gun because there was a racial war going on that I did not have a clue about. As a young man of God, it was not my place to judge him, but rather pray for him.

I looked past his hatred for African Americans and Japanese people. I saw an old man who was telling me his true feelings. At some point, he did not just tell me how he felt, but he indirectly told me to prepare for the racial war that had been going on for a decade and never stopped. Beckwith did not hold his tongue. He was going to say it—regardless of what person was in his presence. The thought went through my mind, "How many white supremacists were living who felt like Beckwith?"

In 2001, I walked into the prison one day and an officer said, "Beckwith died last night."

I looked and asked, "What happened?"

He said, "He died in his sleep."

I instantly shook my head in a state of shock. I always thought he would have changed before he died. During all of my conversations with him, he never changed his tone about an African American or his feelings towards the Japanese.

On the other hand, Sam Bowers was totally different. He was still getting letters calling him the "Honorable" Sam Bowers. Bowers was a white supremacist in Mississippi during the Civil Rights Movement. He was the co-founder of the White Knights of the Ku Klux Klan. He also became the Imperial Wizard of the Ku Klux Klan. In 1964, he murdered civil rights activists James Chaney, Michael Schwerner, and Andrew Goodman near Philadelphia, Mississippi.

He also murdered Civil Rights leader Vernon Dahmer in Hattiesburg, Mississippi. Bowers was sentenced 32 years and later given a life sentence for the murder of Vernon Dahmer. He died in 2006 in prison. Every night when it was time to give him a tray and do my count, I talked to Bowers. He was so quiet and did not say anything racist. On the outside looking in, you would have never known or expected him to be a part of the White Supremacists unless someone told you.

Every letter he received showed him respect. What I learned from Sam Bowers is that Evil also comes in sheep's clothing. I learned looks can be deceiving. I have learned from Sam Bowers that you would never know who you are talking to or understand a person's true feelings by holding a conversation.

On the contrary, Beckwith spoke his feelings openly and did not care what anyone thought of him. I had several conversations with Beckwith because I wanted to know how his mind operated. I did not agree with his feelings or his words, but I listened to his truth because he did not hide it.

I realized that if someone tells you who he or she is, you do not have to like it, but you know exactly who you are dealing with. Therefore, you can treat that person accordingly.

Bowers was the total opposite of Beckwith. Bowers carried himself like he did not have a racist bone in his body, but he was recognized as an elite Ku Klux Klan leader.

Another inmate who stood out was named Joseph, a 13-year-old boy who was in prison for killing his friend by mistake with a gun. I saw him walking through the awful hallways. Joseph looked really scared and bothered. He also looked like he was a child away from his mother and in the cage with vicious lions.

One day I went and got Joseph out his jail cell and talked to him about life. I really felt that I was in a place where I could help him get his mind right, but it was too late to keep him from the felony conviction.

I analyzed what I was doing and wondered how I could support the young men who were lost. I decided to go back to school while working in the prison system to get my master's degree and my doctorate in psychology, with dreams of one day opening up a program to help troubled youth. My influences and testimonies that I had could help, and maybe save, someone's life one day. I knew if I educated myself and could lead by example, I could have an even more inspirational impact on helping others.

Wakeup Call

I had to do a black and white count every night while working in the prison system. Meanwhile, as I was still doing my daily duties at the prison, I noticed something that disturbed me.

I recognized that every night when I did my black and white count, the numbers usually were around the range of 5 Whites to 43 Blacks. I noticed that African Americans were still at the poverty level. African Americans have always been the majority population in prison but are in the minority in the country's population. This woke me up to life as a black man.

Never Hold Grudges

One hot night my brother, Johnny, came to Jackson with some of our friends from Chicago. I was mad because Johnny did not come by the house to see me. The next weekend Johnny and I were riding, and I got smart with him because he did not call me the week before. A week later, Johnny called me and said that Tate, a female friend, had said to call her. I told him that I'd already spoken to her, and I said it with an attitude.

That Tuesday night, Big Ma called me and left me a message saying, "Johnny was fishing and jumped in the lake to save his best friend, and both of them drowned." I jumped in my car and drove fast as I could with my emergency lights on until I got to Lexington.

I ran into Big Ma's house looking for my brother. I said, "Big Ma! What happened?"

She said, "They at the nasty small lake in the country." The closer I got to the small lake, the harder my humming heart was beating. I saw red and blue shining lights as I pulled up to the small lake.

I was looking around and screaming, "What happened?" and "Where is my brother?"

The police officer pulled me to the side and said, "We've been searching all night and we have not found him yet. Go home and get some rest and we will do our best to find him." I listened to the officer.

They finally found Johnny in the lake and pronounced him dead. I wanted to blame someone! I had so much anger and rage in me, but there was no one to accuse. I was clueless, scared, and extremely emotional that night.

I felt like someone had snatched all of my insides out of me and I had no energy to express myself. I went home that night and took a walk with Johnny's 8-year-old son, Quamaine. I remember telling him that I was going to take care of him, and I did. I went into the room to talk to my mother and she had her head face-down. I asked her a question, and she looked up at me with a blank stare. I left out of the room without saying anything.

My mother was broken, empty, and afraid. My mother's heart was broken, and I could not fix it or make the pain go away. My three sisters were extremely hurt and sad during the week of Johnny's funeral. They could not understand why this had happened; there was no one to blame.

My father always sat in the back room watching TV. He called me in the room that week of my brother's funeral. He told me, "You are smart and intelligent. It is proven because you have jumped hurdles other young men have not, you've faced different adversity and succeeded by graduating from college with honors and changing your life around. I want you to look out for your mother and protect your sisters."

He also looked me in my eyes and said, "I am here if you need me."

My older brother James was mad at the world and did not know how to express his feelings. James was always saying, "I miss my brother." James was the oldest out of all my siblings, and he took it hard.

James used to get fighting mad, but this time, there was no one to fight. This fight was for God to heal my family. I felt like I was robbed, with nothing left. Everything I knew and loved was falling apart.

Johnny was the third-born child who demonstrated strength, unity, structure, and leadership. He was not the oldest, but he was the most rational and logical-thinking person I have ever met.

Johnny always thought things through with a plan. Anytime something happened, he always said, "Do you have a plan? And if you have a plan, how are you going to execute it effectively?"

The day before his funeral, I just stayed by myself and did a lot of deep thinking. I thought about two situations where my brother had saved my life. The first situation was when he joined the gang and became the leader to protect me from becoming another statistic of gang violence. Johnny was a deep-thinking brother whom everyone respected wherever he went.

The second incident was when the gang members were following me. The next day I was sitting on top of their car ready to pull the trigger. Johnny said something so ironic, but so wise, to me. He asked me, "Is this the guy that said something to you?"

When I told him no, Johnny told me to get off of his car and find the person who had been talking to me. Johnny did not tolerate ignorance and foolishness. He was 27 years old when he died.

I thought about how to be an effective leader after Johnny died, but I realized I could not walk a mile in his shoes. I had to wear my own shoes and use the wisdom he passed down to be there for my family. I wished a thousand times that I could have told him to take those boots off before he tried to save his friend.

I learned that knowing information and being detailed is so imperative; one small mistake in a second can be extremely detrimental. I wish I could bring him back, but I cannot. I lost my leader, a friend, and a brother.

I still walk around with inner pain because I never got a chance to apologize to Johnny for being angry over something so petty. I learned when my brother Johnny died that we should never hold grudges because life is precious, and anything can happen in a blink of an eye. I still live with it until this day, wishing I could have one more opportunity to convey my thoughts to him.

I used my positive energy to take care of my nephews Sidney and Quamaine along with my daughter, Precious. Every summer and on holidays they were with me. Sidney was six years old and my daughter Precious was five years old. They all looked up to me. Sidney and

Quamaine called me "Uncle P."

Last Conversation

As time passed, Big Ma was getting sick. I went home one hot summer night, and Big Ma told me that someone had bought her some fruits and she was happy. I left and got halfway out of town and remembered that I forgot to give Big Ma some money.

I went back to her house and sat down. She looked up at me with her pretty brown eyes and told me how much she had been missing me. She also told me how much she had been praying for me.

I walked and got into my truck and Levy got in the truck laughing. Levy had some Hennessey in his hand. I asked Levy how long he had been out of prison. He said, "About a week. I prayed every day to get out of prison to see Big Ma before she dies."

I said, "I understand Levy. Keep your head up, Bro'."

Levy said, "Let's go to the store so I can get some ice and a sprite to chase this Hennessey." I reached in my pocket to start my truck up and I did not have my keys.

I asked Levy to go up to Big Ma's house and see if he could find my keys. Levy said okay and jumped out the truck and walked up to Big Ma's house. A few minutes later, Levy came back running and laughing, saying, "I think your grandmother got your keys!"

So, I walked back up to her house and said, "Big Ma, do you have my keys?"

She looked at me directly in my eyes with a beautiful glow and smile. Then she grabbed both of my hands extremely tightly and gave me my keys. I think this was her way of getting to see my face one more time.

Now that I think about it, it was the last time I saw her. Big Ma died that month. My little cousin found her passed out on the floor.

Police Surprise One

The night of Big Ma's funeral, I was driving to my mother's house with tears in my eyes when a car hit my truck from the back. I got out of the truck and saw there were five young men in the car. I called the police instantly. A black police officer showed up and said, "Have you been drinking because your eyes are red?"

I stated, "No sir." He then told me to move my car out the road. The young man's mother arrived at the accident scene. She had her police uniform on, and they had called another officer. Another white officer came to the accident scene. He was short and weighed about 280 pounds.

The short officer snatched me out the truck and threw me on the back seat of the car. He said, "Why are your eyes red?"

I said, "My grandmother's funeral was today, and I am hurting, my Big Ma is gone," with tears running down my face uncontrollably.

The short officer replied, "I do not give a s**t about your grandmother." He then looked back at me and said, "You going to jail!"

My mother and father came and got me out of jail that night. About two months later, I had to go to court for a DUI refusal. Before the court started, my mother walked by me and anointed my head with holy oil and walked off.

Once court started, the original officer, who had arrived at the scene first said, "He did not smell like alcohol, he was not drunk, and the reason I had questioned the driver was that his eyes were bloodshot red." Then, he stated, "I told him to move his truck on the side of the road because it did not appear that he was intoxicated."

The ambulance driver had to testify second. "He was normal, and it did not appear he was drinking."

Finally, the third officer had to testify. The third officer was the short, white officer who cursed me out and slammed me on the car and took me to jail. He said, "Your Honor, this young man was drunk, disrespectful, cursing, and could not walk." I could not believe the officer stood up in court and lied so badly! It showed, because his story was incongruent with the ambulance driver and the story that the original officer who came to the accident scene told.

The judge called all parties into the courtroom. He shouted, "Please do not bring any nonsense in his courtroom again!" Then he slammed the gavel and announced, "NOT GUILTY."

I felt such relief after that day. I was so hurt because of my Big Ma's death, and then to be falsely accused of being drunk ... I was the one who called the police that night to come to the scene of the accident. It is so easy to get put in the system as an African American male because of the stigma people have put on us.

Positive Energy

Life hit me super hard during that time. I worried and wept daily about my Big Ma and Johnny. I continuously regenerated my energy by focusing on my two nephews and my daughter Precious. They were smart and good children.

However, my two hilarious nephews were always plotting and planning how to make me act silly.

I came home early from work one day and asked Sidney and Quamaine what were they up to, and they both hesitated and said,

"Nothing, Uncle P!" at the same time. I knew there was something fishy. They had just put some girls out of the house, and I'd smelled Black & Mild nasty smoke throughout the apartment.

I sat both of them down and had a long educational talk with them about manhood. Sidney and Quamaine were like my sons. Raising Precious, Sidney, and Quamaine introduced me to adulthood really fast!

Police Surprise Two

I was in Jackson on a hot night listening to Ice Cube rocking my head, and the police stopped me. I noticed some blue lights behind me, and I swerved. The police turned on the siren and called over their radio, "Pull over!"

I pulled over slowly, and the cop approached the car, I was petrified, and he called for backup. The police said, "Can you step out of the car, Mister?" I stepped out the car, and he began to search me. I didn't have any weapons. He said, "Sir, where are you going this time of the night?"

I replied, "To my friend Brian's house."

He said, "Give me your license." I gave him my license. He checked it and said, "Put your hands behind your back." He put the handcuffs on me and put me in the back of the police car. "Your licensed is suspended, and your tag is outdated." I did not know my license had been suspended.

As I was getting in the car, I saw several lights. Then, I sat down in the backseat of the police car. I looked up and the officer was standing outside talking to Tod. Tod was the young man that my friend Marcus shot in high school. I said, in the back of my head, "I'm going to jail for sure now."

Tod bent over and looked at me, then he looked at the officer and said, "Let him go." Tod then pulled me out of the car and asked who could come and pick me up.

I said, "My cousin Curtis." Curtis came and got me and the next day I got my license and tag back in excellent standards. I learned the true meaning of forgiveness through Tod.

Tod could have easily held a grudge against me after being in intensive care, but he actually showed true character of how Christ wants us to live. He demonstrated forgiveness, helpfulness, and support to me. I went home and realized that I cannot hold grudges against anyone and that I must also demonstrate forgiveness through my actions.

I had graduated with my master's degree at this time and had started to work at a nearby college. That's where I met a young lady named Brianna. Brianna was a Delta. She had smooth skin and a round face, gray eyes, and was around 5'7" tall. She was a sight to see. We did everything together. Brianna was my best friend and girlfriend.

Everything was going well until Brianna started to feel like I was spending too much time with my fraternity brothers. Brianna and I were a couple that laughed and had fun daily. One windy night, Brianna and I went to a fraternity party and I felt like I was on Cloud Nine.

I had a pretty, foxy young lady on my side with a few extra dollars in my pocket. I thought I was the man. Brianna stayed in the club and I was outside the club talking to three of my fraternity brothers—E. Jackson, Big Rub and Bynum. They went into the club and I stayed outside to take a smoke.

As I was walking in the club, I noticed about 20 football players at the door. They were saying, "Let us in the club!" My fraternity brothers had already had an altercation with the football players before this night. At this time, I was the only brother outside the club from my fraternity. I had been drinking.

The football players started talking crazy and then the commotion started. One of the football players ran towards me quickly as I headed back in the club. I felt something hit my head. I blacked out. Once I became conscious, I realized I was lying in a puddle of blood.

I jumped up, trying to help my fraternity brothers fight the football players, but I felt myself getting weaker as the blood kept running down my face. I noticed that my girlfriend, Brianna, was throwing chairs, screaming and fighting trying to get to me. Finally, my friends threw me in the car and rushed me to the hospital.

The doctor told me after he stitched me up that I would have died if the cut was one inch deeper. He said, "I was a blessed young man."

After leaving the hospital the next morning, my friend told me that he had hit me by mistake, and it had not been a football player. I forgave him and moved forward with my life. It seemed like I was a magnet to trouble, but God always provided a way for me. That day, I talked to Brianna and told her that I wanted better for us and for our life.

I went in my back room and did some self-reflection to make sure I never succumb myself to the same situation again. Once I learned how to love God, I learned how to love others. Once I learned God's principals and how I am governed by those principals, I understood the laws of treating others with kindness and respect. I started spending time with God daily.

Summary (Expression): Forgiveness

"If we confess our sins, he is faithful and just to forgive us our sins and to cleanse us from all unrighteousness." (1 John 1:9)

God is loyal. I always asked God for mental strength through all my situations. I never stopped praying no matter what situation I was faced with. I always made God my number one source for any answers I needed. I felt like I was on the edge and I had to draw close to God and develop an intimate relationship with him. I have learned to admit my wrongdoing and know that God is loyal, faithful, forgiving and steadfast.

CHAPTER 8

EMOTIONAL INTERNAL PAIN

"For I know the plans I have for you," declares the LORD," Plans to prosper you and not to harm you, plans to give you hope and a future." (Jeremiah 29:11)

Brianna came to me one cold rainy night and said she had a job in Montgomery, Alabama. I was upset, but I told her that if she wanted to go that I would support her and move there later. It was that day that our love grew apart. I soon moved to Alabama to be with Brianna, but we had grown apart because of the distance. I moved back to Jackson for two years. I prayed for a better job and God answered my prayers as always.

I received a call one day from my old supervisor in Alabama asking me to come back to Montgomery to work. She said she would double my stunning salary. I was happy and I accepted the offer.

It was the summer of 2006, and I was at a party and met a pretty young lady named Jennifer. She smelled like a rose and looked like a million bucks. I was in love the moment I set eyes on her. Jennifer was smart, pretty, and quick on her feet. She was every man's dream girl.

She moved to Montgomery and things happened fast. We got married a year later. We had two beautiful children, Madison and Jeremiah. I hung out with my fraternity brothers often, but my foundation was God. I became a young Deacon in a nearby Baptist church.

Finally, things were looking very promising to me. I had a new job counseling young men and women in the community. One windy morning, my mother called me and said, "Your brother James died on the bus last night."

I said, "What happened?"

She said, "He had a heart attack while riding the bus in Chicago. When the bus driver made it to the last stop on 95th street in Chicago, he told James to wake up, and he did not respond." She paused, then added, "It was on the news."

I was thinking, "Not again! I cannot take any more heart-breaking news!"

Two years later, I started my own business counseling youth. One day, I had issues getting onto my network. I was locked out of all of my accounts. I could not get into any of my programs.

All of my school work and emails had been compromised. Every time I attempted to open up a new email account, it locked me out again. My passwords did not work. I was upset, but there wasn't anything I could do at that miserable moment but pray.

I was working on my doctorate in psychology at this time. I could not do any of my work for school because all of my information was missing. I was frustrated and hurting to the max.

Jennifer and I had confrontations, and she left and went back to Mississippi. I was thinking, "When it rains, it pours."

I went without lights for weeks, no money for weeks, and no work for weeks. One day I came home, and my car had broken down, my cable had been cut off, and my lights were off. When my birthday came around, and I was alone in the dark. I called my fraternity brother, Big Rueb, who believes in feeding everyone with positive energy.

He stated, "It is your birthday, Big Homie! A year from now, you won't even be thinking about this situation." He also said, "Keep living and keep feeding the atmosphere positive energy and it will come back to you."

I said, "I got you, Bro'."

He then added, "You need to write a book because you've got a story that needs to be told." I laughed. He said, "Oh yeah, I almost forgot to ask you, have you been to the mailbox yet?"

I said, "No," laughing. I told him to hold on and went to the mailbox. I opened the mailbox slowly and found an envelope with Big Rueb's name on it. There was one hundred dollars inside. I went back to the phone and thanked him.

He said, "Big Bro', you going to be good. Keep living!" And then he hung up the phone up.

That conversation with Big Rueb on that lonely confused day gave me the extra boost I needed to keep living and fighting. The next day, I prayed. After that, I read the Bible daily and meditated on God's word. My number one prayer was for God to take everything negative out of my life.

During this stage of my life, I had learned the power of prayer. I had one year to finish my doctorate, but I could not finish because all of the documentation on my computer had been destroyed.

At this moment in my life, I was doing an internship and my supervision for counseling. I had finished all of my supervision hours. I worked for Dr. Danielle in Phoenix City, Alabama and she took total advantage of my situation. She was nice at first, for the most part. After I finished my psychology and counseling hours, I continued to work for her without pay.

A month later, I went by her office and gave her my counseling hours documentation. Then I asked her to please send the papers off after she signed them because I needed them to get to the counseling board as soon as possible. I also mentioned to her that I had been living in my house without any lights. I told her I would have gotten them to her sooner, but that I had been under a lot of pressure.

Coping with Life Situations

Dr. Danielle told me, "I will take care of it!" with a smile.

Then I stated, "Dr. Danielle, I cannot work at your practice anymore because I do not have any money for gas. I need to find some income to put my life back in perspective."

Even though she said, "Okay," I felt something on the inside that told me she was not right. The counseling board never received my paperwork. I called her about my documentation, and she mentioned that she did send them off and she did not have another copy.

I said, "Tell me that again so that I can get a clear understanding."

Then she said, "I do not have your hours in my head. I cannot help you."

I just said, "Thank you" and hung the phone up. Instantly, I got on my knees and started to weep in prayer.

Life Lesson

I asked God to take everything negative out of my life. Instantly, the next day, I started doing community service and helping others. I stopped working on computers for months and read my Bible. My strength was beyond my measure because I started depending on God and not myself.

The storm was still there in my life, but I had to keep moving with a positive outlook. My good friend, Dr. Charles, always came and checked on me. Dr. Charles is a psychologist who I have been working with for many years. He conveyed to me that I had to keep working and stay focused.

I felt that I was in a bad place in my life without any money. I felt like no one wanted to be around me. Little did I know that God knew I needed encouraging people in my presence.

I was almost about to break. I was in a place of losing all hope. In addition to Dr. Charles helping me, my accountant Shabazz, who is a black Hebrew Israelite, would send me Bible verses daily. He would to always come to my office to talk to me and make sure I was doing ok.

I was thinking, "Why are people talking to me? I am in a bad place, and no one wants to be around a person who is broken like me." I had always been a person who gives, but once I was down to my last cent, I felt alone. At times, I felt like I was in the middle of the ocean with no life-jacket and no one was coming for me. I also felt like I had been trying my best to get back to dry land, but the waves just kept pushing me further and further away.

One Thursday afternoon in 2016, I went into the store and asked a man to get in front of me. I offered to buy him something to eat. I had one hundred dollars to my name with a house in foreclosure, but I always felt really good on the inside as long as I was helping someone else.

I grabbed a cup of coffee and poured it into a container. The young man who was working in the store told me he was going to pay for the coffee, and he walked away really fast. I walked to my car and prayed to God with supplication. I was so thankful for that one cup of coffee.

The next day, I went into my office. A short time later, my accountant came into my office with a thousand-dollar check. He told me that it was my money and I did not have to pay him back. He also said, "God told me to give it to you."

I had not asked him for anything, and I was shocked. I was grateful. As long as I have known Shabazz, he has never spoken about his religion or anyone else's faith. He did not talk about going to church, nor did he criticize me or anyone else. He demonstrated the presence of God within himself by treating me like he wanted to be treated. He saw a brother that needed an extra boost.

One night I was looking at a bottle of liquor to drink and Shabazz texted me with a quote from Scripture. Right then, I put the bottle down and read God's word.

During this time, my car had broken down. I decided to go to walk to Starbucks that morning. I began to talk to God. I said, "God this is not like you. I cannot go to church on Sunday!"

Instantly, after that, God spoke to my spirit, "The church is in you, and you bring the Word to the church!"

I kept walking in a shock. I got to Starbucks and sat down. A young man named Tom came over and asked me, "Do you have the number to the bus station?"

I said, "Sure." Then, I asked Tom if he was hungry.

He said, "Yes!" Then, I reached in my pocket and gave Tom a couple of dollars. I told him to go across the street to Walmart and buy something to shave with because his hair was all over his face. Meanwhile, I went to Zaxby's and got him something to eat. Once he arrived back from Walmart, I had his food.

Tom sat down and I asked him if I could pray with him before we ate. Tom said, "Yes." I prayed and then Tom began to eat his meal and tell me how he had gotten into his situation. He mentioned that he had been staying in a shelter for a couple of days. He also stated that he had been in jail for some misdemeanor violations.

I then asked him to elaborate more. He started talking about how he had been going through a lot from his past relationship with his baby's mother. After talking to Tom, he seemed like a nice person who was going through hard times. He mentioned that he had to leave. I asked Tom, "Why you are leaving so early?"

He looked at me and said, "I got to go before 8:30 p.m. because the hospital doors will lock at a particular time." Tom stated, "I need somewhere warm to sleep because I do not have anywhere to sleep for the night."

I told him that I understood, and I gave him a few dollars to get something to eat later. He thanked me, then we prayed and parted ways.

After Tom left, I felt terrible. I had been complaining that I did not have any lights on in my house at the time. However, Tom did not have anywhere to live. I felt so good helping him; it helped me understand that we all have some storms in our lives. I learned that it is how we deal with the storm that makes us strong.

Weeks later, I went to Jackson to visit my parents. My mother, father, and I went to Enterprise to rent a car. We laughed and talked like it was a good day.

The next day when I got ready to go back to Alabama, my mother and father were standing outside waving at me. My father asked me, "Do you have any money?"

I said, "I have a little money, but not a lot."

He reached into his pocket and got a crispy twenty-dollar bill out of his wallet and gave it to me. After that, he said, "Be careful."

About midnight, my mother called me and said, "Your father is sitting on the stairs, and we cannot get a pulse." He was pronounced dead about an hour later.

I cried in my bed rocking back and forth, saying, "God, let Your Will be done." I knew at that moment that my life belonged to God and He had to guide me. I was so hurt to see my mother, sisters, children, nieces, and nephews go through another tragic moment. My mother asked me several times what had gone wrong that day. I never had an answer for her.

I was hurt, but it could not compare to the internal pain my mother was going through. My mother had been married to my father for 47 years. They operated as one. My mother's pain still runs deep. She has lost a mother, two sons, and a husband. Lord, have mercy!

I was clueless about what had happened. For days up until my father's funeral, I remembered those words he told me when Johnny died: "I want you to look out for your mother and protect your sisters."

People were telling me to be strong for my mother and sisters. Those words were easy to hear but applying them to my life was almost impossible because I had a hurt that ran deeper than the ocean with no edges. I had a pain that no one could see. I had mixed feelings no one could touch. I had dreams that no one can imagine.

My only strength at this point was God. God helped me to realize that I was surrounded with brothers in my fraternity who loved and respected me. God allowed me to understand that I had brothers I was raised with who were there for me. Sly and Brian were my childhood friends who were right there to help me through those painful moments. Sly preached an excellent sermon at my father's funeral.

I had friends and fraternity brothers, but Johnny, Big Ma, James, and my father could not be replaced. As months passed, I realized that I had to figure out a way to lead my family and keep things in the right perspective. I did not ask for this position; God put me in this position to be a wise leader for my family.

This situation was so scary because I had depended on James, Johnny, and my father for guidance. I felt so alone, hurt, and helpless for my family and for myself. I am the last man standing, and I have learned to be the peacemaker and think rationally through all situations with God through Jesus Christ as my navigation system.

I had to learn God's word and seek Him through all circumstances. God became my rock and His son, Jesus, is my Salvation in Whom I trust.

I learned to be territorial like the lion. I had to instantly go into protection mode to be there for my family by setting a positive example, being a peacemaker, and living as a God-fearing man. I am my brother's keeper and I will forever be.

Walking Away from Danger

I learned to think rationally, like an elephant. When an elephant hears danger coming its way from hunters with guns on the attack, it understands their language and moves to another location. If the sound were coming from a group of individuals who were not hunting it, the elephant does not change its position.

I've had to learn to walk away from danger. In my family, my wisdom, mindset, and leadership are needed. I've had to learn not to react so fast because if something happens to me, it would have a pyramid effect. I have had to learn to exclude myself from the petty nonsense behaviors.

I've had to learn how to be a problem-solver in my family, and not a hot-headed person. I've had to learn not to always to attempt to solve a situation with a gun or my fist. I have had to learn how to fight with my mind by reading, teaching, educating, seeking God, and never fearing man. I have had to learn to fear God and to ask Him to teach me how to discern right from wrong because I cannot lead any task without his guidance. **God is my STRONGHOLD**.

Summary (Expression): Emotional Internal Pain

Consequently, we should overcome situations by putting the pieces together one minute at a time. Jesus tells us not to worry. Therefore, putting our worries on Jesus and doing our best and striving to be upright is ultimately challenging, but we have to follow the commandment of God and make every effort to treat each person how we want to be treated. If we stay steadfast, we will be blessed in any situation we will encounter. For instance, take Joseph in the Bible. Joseph was in a pit, and he was favored, Joseph was in slavery, and he was favored, Joseph was in prison, and he was favored, and Joseph was the second man in charge of Egypt, and he was favored. Providing that, you see, as long as Joseph was upright, the Most-High favored him. Do right regardless of your situation and watch how you will shine like a light in the darkness. We have to be different and see things from a Godly perspective.

CHAPTER 9
BACK TO THE BASICS

Rebuilding from the Bottom

We have to strategize a plan and follow the rules to overcome our generational bondage since slavery. The fear of not succeeding, the fear of someone laughing at our ideals, and the fear that it won't work will keep us in bondage.

God be the Glory

God be the glory; I earned my doctorate in psychology and continued my life to help other young men in my outreach ministry and counseling program. I used my revelations, experiences, and education to help young adults to improve their life situations.

Throughout my life, I have lived on the Edged and kept pushing through all adversity, regardless of what circumstances appeared. There are so many young men and women that are trapped in society, and they have no clue how to navigate through the adversities of life.

It is tough to deal with the police, remain uneducated, and live in poverty while trying to make it out of a revolving cycle. We have to change our mindset by reading, keeping smart individuals around us, and making God our number one foundation. God always answered my prayers, and He will answer yours. We have to believe, work, and stand on God's Word (the Truth).

Treating people with love and loving God with all our heart is what He requires. We have to educate, teach, and govern ourselves accordingly. We have to govern our communities and protect our families and our loved ones. Exposing individuals to new information enhances our thought processes to a conscious state of mind where we can do better.

When all things look cloudy and you cannot bear any more pain, regardless of your circumstance or your situation, keep moving, keep fighting, keep grinding, and do not look back.

Our mind tells us that we will be in a particular condition forever; we have to dismiss any negative thoughts that will keep us in bondage. Stop looking at problems and find solutions to our questions.

Worrying won't change anything. You have to be tired of living a certain way and willing to make the necessary steps to change your lifestyle, even if you are living life on the edge.

My story started in 1974. With the grace of God through Jesus Christ, I was able to endure the death of my best friend (Larry), the death of my father, the death of my grandmother (Big Ma), two brothers' deaths, a horrible divorce (dealing with life's failures), and many other obstacles. Through adversity, God opened my eyes to see the possibility within myself. I am blessed with a spirit of endurance, prayer, and a great support system. God is my Rock through His precious Son, Jesus Christ. AMEN

A quote from Og Mandino can best describe my ongoing journey through life: "*I will persist until I succeed. Always will I take another step. If that is of no avail, I will take another, and yet another. In truth, one step at a time is not too difficult. I know the small attempts, repeated, will complete any undertaking.*"

"Living my life on the edge" represents fearing God and always wanting to please Him in all situations. As long as my edge is fearing God, I will always have knowledge. His Will is my number one objective.

"The fear of the LORD is the beginning of knowledge, but fools despise wisdom and instruction." (New International Version
Proverbs 1:7)

Thank you for allowing me to share *Mississippi Dreams: Living Life on the Edge*—From the street life to getting to know Christ.

Characters no longer here with us

- Sweet was murdered in St. Louis during a robbery.

- Johnny (my brother) drowned trying to save his friend. As a man, Johnny taught me so much and always were there for me. I still dream about my big brother until this day. Love you Bro'.

- James (my oldest brother) died of a heart attack. James would give you his shirt off of his back. I love you big Bro'.

- Johnny Sr. (my father, also known as "Hook") died of a heart attack. I am so thankful for my Earthly father who God blessed me with for a short time. Daddy always knew the words to say at the right time. I miss you, Daddy.

- Big MA (my grandmother) died of a heart attack. She kept her word and left me that shotgun house in her will. Big Ma had an unconditional love for me. I miss you, Big Ma.

Characters in the book—what are they doing now?

- Brian (also known as "my brother from another mother") is working two jobs. He has a beautiful wife and a son named Jalen who is in college and is playing football for the University of

Idaho.

- Kelly (also known as Kevin) got a life sentence in prison and got out 18 years later. Kevin is currently working at a barbershop and at a plant in Jackson. Kevin has demonstrated true rehabilitation.

- Brianna is living in Atlanta and working hard. She has two beautiful children. We still communicate as friends.

- Tod (also known as Mike) is a detective on the police force in Jackson. Tod and I became friends later and never brought the incident between us up again.

- Dr. Charles is currently working as a psychologist in Montgomery. He still comes by my house and checks on me. Dr. Charles is well-grounded and always thinking rationally. He continues to dedicate his life to encouraging others.

- Curtis (my cousin) is working as an officer in the U.S. Military. He still dedicates his life to giving back to others.

- Marzette is a captain at the fire department. Marzette calls me every other day to laugh because he knows I am going to say something hilarious.

- Christine is currently living in Lexington, Mississippi and is working hard.

- Precious (my precious daughter) graduated from Mississippi State University and is pursuing her career as a physical therapist.

- Jennifer (my first ex-wife) is doing extremely well taking care of my two loving children. Jennifer is in a committed relationship and we co-parent sincerely well.

- Coop (my friend) is a police officer in Jackson. Coop is a great person who will push you that extra mile, both in as an athlete and as a person. He is a great basketball player.

- Shabazz (my accountant) owns his own accounting firm and constantly demonstrates uplift daily. Shabazz is a deep brother who does his best to keep individuals on a positive path.

- Sly (also known as Tyrone) is preaching God's word. Tyrone is on radio stations and has his own gospel TV show.

- Quamaine (my nephew) went to Jackson State University. He is currently living in Memphis and is working hard at Amazon with his fiancé and two children. When I go through things, Quamaine also gives me the same advice I gave him growing up. Oh, how times have changed! I am always appreciative that God allowed me to be a part of his life.

- Sidney (my nephew) graduated from Mississippi Valley State

University with his bachelor's degree and master's degree. He also joined Omega Psi Phi Fraternity and is currently living in Houston and working at a college. It was an honor to help my sister to raise him.

- Tina (my sister) is the oldest of my siblings who I truly love and I am forever thankful that she allowed me to be a part of my nephew's life.

- Tab (my sister) is my number one supporter. We talk daily and laugh about the small things in life. Tab motivates me daily. She called me one morning around 3 a.m. to ask me "What is the most powerful thing you can do?" and then hung up. She is always keeping me on my toes.

- Princess (my baby sister) is my ace in the hole. We talk each morning before she goes to work. Stay focused, Little Sister!

- Barbara (my sweet mother) is currently living in Jackson and is the Rock of the family since my father died. She is as sweet as pie. My mother is always telling me to do what is right, to fight with kindness, and to follow God's word.

- Cle is a productive young man in Lexington and is working hard in the construction field.

- Princess, Tab, and Tina (my sisters) are my biggest support system.

- Big Reub (Ace) is working hard in Dallas, TX with a beautiful wife and child. Thanks, Big Reub, for believing in me and constantly reminding me that my life is a story. Keep on keeping on.

Thank You

Thank you for reading my story. Hopefully, this book has inspired someone to be true to themselves, to make God their foundation, and to never give up regardless of their circumstances.

References

Ersche KD, *et al.* (2012) Abnormal brain structure implicated in stimulant drug addiction. Science 335:601–604.

Nestler, E. J. (2001), Molecular Neurobiology of Addiction. The American Journal on Addictions, 10: 201-21

Made in the USA
Lexington, KY
05 November 2019